Also Known As Harper

Also Known As
HARPER

ANN HAYWOOD LEAL

HENRY HOLT AND COMPANY

NEW YORK

Henry Holt and Company, LLC
Publishers since 1866
175 Fifth Avenue
New York, New York 10010
www.HenryHoltKids.com

Library of Congress Cataloging-in-Publication Data
Leal, Ann Haywood.
Also known as Harper / Ann Haywood Leal.—1st ed.
p.   cm.
Summary: Writing poetry helps fifth-grader Harper Lee Morgan cope
with her father's absence, being evicted, and having to skip school to care
for her brother while their mother works, and things look even brighter
after she befriends a mute girl and a kindly disabled woman.
ISBN-13: 978-0-8050-8881-6
ISBN-10: 0-8050-8881-4
[1. Single-parent families—Fiction.   2. Family problems—Fiction.
3. Brothers and sisters—Fiction.   4. Poets—Fiction.   5. Selective
mutism—Fiction.   6. People with disabilities—Fiction.]   I. Title.
PZ7.L46327Als 2009
[Fic]—dc22
2008036940

First Edition—2009
Book designed by April Ward
Printed in the United States of America on acid-free paper. ∞
1   3   5   7   9   10   8   6   4   2

For my dad, Lionel Haywood,
and in loving memory of
my mom, Peggy Haywood—
my first readers

Also Known As Harper

Chapter One

WINNIE RAE EARLY followed ten steps behind me the entire way home from school. It was hard not to fall into rhythm with the noisy sniff she took every third step. I knew without turning around that she was doing what she'd done all day long at school, lifting her arm up and wiping at the chapped underside of her nose with the inside of her wrist.

When my toes had just about reached my driveway, she ran ahead of me and across to her yard next door and threw her backpack to the side of her daddy's brown metal toolshed. That old shed sat a good foot over the line on our property, and I swear I'd seen her watching me before from the square cutout window in the side.

The little doors in the front were made to look

like barn doors, and I saw her pull on the long handle in the middle of the *X* and let herself in.

I was tempted to wait at the bottom of my porch and spy on her for once, until I noticed another one of those nasty signs slapped in the middle of my front door.

"It won't do you no good to take it off of there, Harper." Winnie Rae stepped around and hollered at me from beside the shed. "My mama will just come on back and put up another one."

I scrunched up a corner of the sign and threw it in her direction. "You get your tired old sneakers off my property, Winnie Rae, and worry about your own sorry self."

She pointed one chewed-up fingernail in my direction. "It ain't your property anymore, Harper Lee Morgan, according to that sign there."

Winnie Rae was right and I knew it. That sign meant the landlord, who happened to be her mama, was getting ready to kick us out and rent to someone new. Someone who could pay.

I'd heard my mama on the phone last week, trying to borrow some of the rent money. "I just need to get Harper through the fifth grade. I don't want to uproot her in the middle of the school year like this."

But I'd come home from school and seen another sign, plastered up over the scraps of the old one. The time before, they'd put up two, one on the door and one on the front window. This time there was only the one.

As I reached up to pull it the rest of the way off, I could see it was a little different from the others. I made a small, careful rip at the top and tore it slowly down the middle, right between the "N" and the "A" in "FINAL."

The front door swung open, and my little brother hopped on one foot sideways, across the porch. "I broke my leg today, Harper Lee." He bent down and tightened an old yellow hand towel around his knee.

"I can see that, Hemingway." I held the door open for him to hop back inside.

"I tripped over Mama's washrag and fell down a whole half a step." He untied the towel to show me. "There's no blood yet, but it's trying to come out. I can tell."

I let him lean on my arm partway into the kitchen. Then he let go and started hopping on the other leg.

"How long has she been asleep?" I lifted Mama's

sweatshirt from the back of her chair at the kitchen table and set it over her shoulders.

Hemingway sat down at the table and scooted his handwriting workbook toward me. "Since all the way through the capitals and most of the way through the lowercase letters."

I took out my purple marker and made circles around his best letters. "You're getting really good at these," I said. "It's about time you went to putting some of these letters into words. I could maybe teach you to write a story. Six is plenty old enough to write a poem or two."

He smiled and brought one of the purple circles right up to his eyeball. "Mama read me chapter three today." He pointed at her special book sitting all careful like in the middle of a folded-up dish towel. I knew it to be her thirty-seventh reading of *To Kill a Mockingbird*. I had put up the thirty-sixth tally mark on the wall by the refrigerator just two weeks ago. She had timed it perfectly so she'd finish up the last word of the last chapter on my eleventh birthday.

Mama could probably spout out that book from the middle of her heart. She loved it so much, she said it was only natural to give me the name of the author.

I picked up the envelope in the middle of the table.

It was one of the bills that kept coming in the mail. This one was from the electric company. I turned it over and saw Mama's writing, all slanty and perfect across the back of the envelope. When Mama got an idea for one of her stories, she wrote it down on whatever was handy. Her words always traveled right across the paper and made a bright picture in my mind. I picked up her pen and fixed up some of the words. She was forever mixing up "was" and "saw."

Lately, I hadn't been seeing many of her words around. Just a sentence or two, sometimes. Not thick stacks of paper like she used to write.

Mama let out a squeaky breath and lifted her head. She sat back in her chair and rubbed at the bumpy placemat marks on her cheek. "Hey there, Harper Lee. How was school?" She was trying to make her smile all cheerful, but I knew about the worry behind it.

"They put up another sign, Mama." I pulled the scraps out of my pocket and set them down on the table in front of her.

"I'm sorry, Harper." She seemed to be getting ready to cry. "I've gone to work at four-thirty in the morning for the last two weeks, but I haven't been able to get enough together." She let out another squeaky sigh. "I told Mrs. Early I got a whole month's rent, plus a good two-thirds of another, but she said it's all four months or nothing. She said she's got to take care of her own. She can't be letting us stay on for free."

She shook her head. "I tried. I swear, I tried."

Her eyes got all shiny and I knew what was coming, so I got myself out of that kitchen as fast as I could. Mama had been trying to move us into a cheaper place for a couple of months now, but she said it cost more to get a new place than it did for us to stay put where we were. It sure didn't make a whole lot of sense to me. Even so, she was getting a head start on the packing. She said when the time came we might have to move kind of quick like.

I could barely push my door open in my room, it was so jam-packed full of liquor-store boxes. I saw Mama had packed all the long pants from my bottom drawer in a tall whiskey box, and I got to work fixing them.

Sure enough, they were packed in every which way. She used up all her cleaning energy at her housekeeping jobs. Our house was picked up and clean, but it took you an hour to find a pencil in a drawer or a game or a sweater in a closet. Anything she did around our house was always fast, with whatever little bit she had left over.

The red paint on the wooden apple crate looked dry, but I tested it with my pinky finger before I picked it up from the newspapers in the corner of my room.

I opened my middle drawer slowly and carefully lifted out my stacks of paper. My poems and my stories. I wasn't taking any chances of getting them bent up or shoved into a stinky old whiskey box.

I took the stacks out, one at a time, and placed them in the middle of the crate, trying to quiet Daddy's low voice coming up, sideways, in my brain.

I knew you wouldn't live up to your name from the moment your mother insisted on giving it to you. He had tossed my papers down so part of the first page was soaked with the whiskey in his coffee mug. *You don't know squat about weaving together a story, Harper Lee. So you may as well give it up.* And he'd laughed like he'd just told the funniest joke he knew, and he'd poured himself a fresh coffee cup full.

Hemingway stood at my doorway and pushed at a whiskey box with his toe.

"Hey, Hem." I moved a couple of boxes aside so he could come in. "You don't believe in letting a person settle themselves in before you get to bothering them, now, do you?"

But I patted the corner of the bed. Hemingway's company wasn't so bad. He had a way about him that made all the tired go out of a person.

"Mama says we got to move pretty quick here," he said, eyeing all my boxes.

"Not just yet." I straightened up a stack of poems on my bed. "She just wants us to get a head start, is all."

"Thing is . . ." He bit at a hangnail on his thumb and I knew what was coming. Hem always got fidgety when he was thinking about Daddy. "How's he going to find us?"

I pulled his thumb away from his mouth. "He'll find us if the time comes."

I knew how badly Hem wanted Daddy to come walking back up our front steps, and I wanted that for him, I really did. But I wasn't so sure I wanted that for me.

He got up and took a good look out my bedroom window. "It's almost time to go out, Harper Lee."

"You know I'm not going to go out to the porch," I reminded him.

He leaned forward as if he was going to tell me a

good secret. "But I'm thinking I might wait on the driveway path today, right out front, you know? Just so as he can see me better."

But deep down I think Hemingway knew as well as I did, when Daddy had made his way down that driveway path a whole year ago, he had never figured on coming back.

Chapter Two

I STOOD AT THE EDGE of the lawn at the bottom of my porch steps and tried to decide how I was going to move the little peach tree that Hemingway and I had planted a couple years back. There was no way I was going to leave that for Winnie Rae Early to gaze on with her ugly old self.

She leaned up against the shed across the side yard. "My mama said you could set a clock by that pitiful brother of yours, Harper Lee." Winnie Rae's voice got downright whiny when she hollered.

What's your fat old mama know, anyway? I thought.

"My mama said he's just wasting his time on that porch every night. If y'all would've wanted to find your daddy, y'all should've followed the whiskey trail while it was still fresh." Then Winnie Rae took to laughing so hard, I was thinking she might bust open that skinny purple vein that snaked up the side of her forehead. She had the kind of laugh that went silent for a while as she gasped for extra air.

I went in and got a glass of yellow lemonade for Hem. He was one to appreciate a cold drink while he was doing his waiting. It was warm for April, and I was thinking I wouldn't be needing my sweatshirt for much longer.

I handed him the glass and sat down next to him on the bottom step. "Any sign?"

He shook his head and took a slurp off the top of the glass. "It wasn't very comfortable out there on the driveway path. Here you got something to lean yourself on." He tipped his head back against the porch rail and drew an "H" in the water dribbles on the side of his glass. It always seemed extra quiet when Hem was doing his waiting. It was as if everything around him was holding its breath.

Truth was, I knew why Hemingway waited there every night. He was the only one Daddy had been halfway decent to. Even when the whiskey turned his words into slow jumbles, Daddy usually made nice when it came to Hem.

Mama had figured it out straightaway. I remembered sitting on the steps with her, watching Daddy push Hem on his tricycle. *Hem's a boy, plain and simple, Harper Lee. When your daddy looks at Hem, it makes him think of happy times. He reminds Daddy of when he was a boy. But when he looks at us, he just sees the right now, and it reminds him of how his life hasn't turned out anything like he planned.*

"I heard a car 'bout five minutes ago." Hemingway looked off toward the end of the driveway. "Sounded just like Daddy's pickup when it turned the corner." He made like he was turning a steering wheel.

I nodded. Sometimes I got to thinking about Ms. Harper Lee, the author, and how I wished Atticus Finch in her book, *To Kill a Mockingbird,* was my real daddy. I pretended I was Scout Finch, the daughter in the story, and that Hem and me were sitting out there waiting for Atticus to come back from a day of lawyering at the Maycomb County courthouse. He'd ask me about my poems and he'd sit down and read a couple out loud, pausing and thinking about all the really good parts.

But the sight of the Earlys across the way brought me back to my own porch, and I remembered I was

Harper Lee Morgan, daughter of no one who mattered much.

"It ain't polite to stare," Hemingway whispered across the yard. He wasn't like me. He never let himself be out-and-out rude to anyone, even Winnie Rae Early's enormous mother.

Mrs. Early made her way down her steps sideways, her elbow out and tilted at an angle to keep her balance. It looked to be plenty hard to try to move those heavy sausage links sideways and continue the stare going across the yard. On top of it all, she was trying to keep her revival-tent dress from riding up in the back and still hold tight to her pack of cigarettes.

"Going off to smoke her cancer sticks, I guess." I nodded my head toward the end of her driveway.

Winnie Rae said her mother thought that people who smoked and drank inside their own homes were uncivilized and had no proper upbringing. So Mrs. Early went off every night to do her smoking in a lawn chair beside their pickup at the end of their driveway.

"Who's that?" Hem jabbed his little finger in the direction of a woman in the other lawn chair. The webbing sagged down in the middle as if it was reaching for the ground under the woman's seat.

"That's her sister," I said. "Winnie Rae's aunt. You've seen her before. She's the one that drives the green van. She comes around every once in a while and smokes up a few cigarettes with Mrs. Early."

"The one with the little kid." Hem stared down Winnie Rae's cousin, who looked to be about four.

I leaned in close to Hem. "She's looking extra large today." I nodded toward Mrs. Early.

He sat back and tried to make his stomach pooch out in front of him. "She's got a baby in there."

"Huh-uh." I tilted my head to the side to get a different view. "She's just fat."

Hem shook his head. "She's got a baby in there. I heard her tell Mama yesterday."

"Sure hard to tell when a person's that big." I blew a piece of hair out of my eyes. "All we need around here is another Early."

When Mrs. Early finally heaved her big old body down into that lawn chair, I saw her kick at the ground and say a few words into the dirt that I'm not inclined to repeat. Winnie Rae's cousin looked a little off-kilter at first, when Mrs. Early let loose with her swears, but not too out of sorts. He went right back to running his little cars along the dented-up part on the back of the van, as if he was used to those words.

I nudged Hem with the back of my hand. "I see she found my message." I'd gathered up the stubs from all her nasty cigarettes and spelled out *Smoke Kills* on the ground by her chair.

"I'm going to miss them when we go to our new house," I said, shaking my head. "Mean neighbors are much more interesting than the regular old kind."

I'd have taken my time and thought of something more clever to spell out on the ground if I'd known that was going to be the last night in my house.

Chapter Three

SARAH LYNN NEWHART leaned back against the chain-link fence next to the school. She had her arms bent out to her sides like chicken wings, and she had a good backward bounce going on the fence.

"It's about time!" She gave one last bounce and pushed herself up to a stand. Then she moved in to her usual five inches away from my face. That Sarah Lynn was a close talker. It ran in her family.

"You oversleep or something?" I could feel the little bursts of her breath on my chin. "Bell's going to ring in about five minutes."

I took a half a step back. "Hemingway wouldn't get out from under my feet. He wouldn't let me leave until I made a sling for his arm."

"He break his arm?" She reached behind her and pulled a blue rolled-up paper out of a diamond link in the fence.

I shook my head. "You know Hem. The things he wants most in this world are a big white cast and a pair of crutches."

She held the blue paper out to me. "Hot off the press. I grabbed you one from Mrs. Rodriguez's desk before Winnie Rae Early snapped them all up for herself."

I unrolled the paper, and my stomach got the prickly churns.

"It's just like last year." I sat down on the bottom of the playground slide and smoothed the paper open over my legs.

She shrugged. "Just like last year?"

I nodded. "The paper. It's exactly the same. Word for word."

I had memorized every letter of that paper last year, I had been so excited about it. And just then the words from the blue paper came into my mind before my eyes had even gotten to them. I was going to get another chance to read my poems, and I could feel that same tingly feeling in the front of my head that I always got when my words arranged themselves into a poem or a story.

But it was hard to push away the memory of Daddy sitting at the kitchen table with the whiskey poisoning the air around him. *You're lazy with a pen, Harper Lee. Being sloppy with your words is the worst kind of lazy. If you expect me to sign my name to this sort of garbage, you got another think coming.* And then he'd put the tip of his pen on top of the "P" on the Whaley County Poetry Contest permission slip, like he might be getting ready to sign his name, anyway. But the tip of his pen had pressed down harder, and hadn't let up until it had made a big crooked "X" over the front of my permission slip and edged over onto one of my poems.

I tried to remind myself that Daddy and his green-ink pen weren't anywhere near me anymore.

"What's wrong, Harper Lee?" Sarah Lynn, who was crouched down by the slide, moved in so her nose was practically touching mine.

I shrugged. "Nothing. Just thinking about the poems I've been working on." But I couldn't push that voice out of my head. It made me feel like Daddy was back with us again. He had always tried to make my poems shrivel up and seem like they weren't anything special. Nothing that you'd read out loud at a poetry contest.

I scooted back and put the blue paper in my backpack, trying to remember his words couldn't reach me. "Maybe you could come over and we could work on our poems this afternoon."

"Huh-uh." She shook her head. "You know we can just be school friends."

A school friend was like a secret you could never share with anyone. I wanted a real best friend.

"My daddy hasn't even lived at our house for a good solid year now," I reminded her.

She shook her head again, slow and hard with each word. "Mama says no way am I to go to your house ever again. I'm not even allowed on your street." She raised her eyebrows. "For heaven's sake, Harper Lee. I'm not even supposed to be talking to you at school."

If I had done something wrong, it would be so easy. I could say I was sorry and we could be best friends again. But it didn't seem to work that way when you were trying to apologize for someone else. For something someone else had done.

I stood up. "Your mama could drive you and pick you up herself."

"Not a chance." She pressed her lips together hard.

I nodded and breathed out a long breath of air. Sarah Lynn's mama had never gotten over the time Daddy gave Sarah Lynn a ride home from our house. Mama was at work, and Daddy had been refilling his coffee cup all afternoon. By the time he went to drive Sarah Lynn home, he'd emptied a good three-quarters of his whiskey bottle.

When he'd tried to back out of Sarah Lynn's driveway, he'd plowed over the better portion of Mrs. Newhart's cutting garden and sent their garbage cans skidding into the neighbor's driveway across the street. Afterward, Daddy had had trouble making his eyes focus right and didn't seem to care one way or the other about all the yelling Mrs. Newhart was doing. She'd called Mama at work and really let her have it. Mrs. Newhart said you could smell the whiskey in the air a good ten-foot circle around him.

I made my face like I didn't care. "Maybe Mrs. Rodriguez will give us some time in class today." I swung my backpack over my shoulder and went to get in line on the four-square court.

I planted my feet along a thick painted edge of a square and tried to push Daddy out of my brain.

Once his whiskey smell had gotten in somewhere, it took some doing to air it out.

Sarah Lynn nudged her way behind me and bumped up against the books on my back. Her long sleeves swished against the canvas of my bag as she bent over to tie her shoe.

I looked down at her. "Could you take a couple of steps back, please?" I pointed behind me. "You're going to squash my lunch."

I liked Sarah Lynn and I wanted to be more than just school friends, but sometimes she just plain annoyed me. I wanted to be the kind of friends that had sleepovers and rode their bikes in each other's driveways. There wasn't anything so special about the flowers in her mama's cutting garden, anyway. And I'd taken a million whiskey drives with Daddy. I was an expert at it. I'd taught Sarah Lynn how to get a good knuckle grip on the seat so you wouldn't slide around too much in back.

Winnie Rae stepped out of line a few people ahead of me and turned around so she could get a good nosy stare going. "My mama said you shouldn't have ripped that sign down." Her yellow T-shirt rode up in the front, and I could see a white stripe of skin trying to fold itself over the waist of her jeans. "She doesn't have time to be putting those things back up. She's too busy running the motel."

I rolled my eyes and nudged Sarah Lynn in the leg, softly, with my heel. "Winnie Rae wants us to think that her mama's a front-desk hostess, taking people's reservations and such."

Sarah Lynn raised one eyebrow and looked in Winnie Rae's direction.

I made my voice a little louder, so it carried up the line. "But anyone at all knows the truth, Sarah Lynn."

Sarah Lynn gave a good evil eye to Winnie Rae for me.

"She might be a landlord." I added a good evil eye of my own. "But she's just a housekeeper. Same as my mama." The bell was going to ring any second, so I had to move fast. I had a lot more words trying to spill out of my mouth at Winnie Rae.

"And another thing you should know, Sarah Lynn." I stepped out of line myself, so Winnie Rae would be sure to hear me. "My mama does laundry and floors and such in people's houses, but I know Mrs. Early to be more of a toilet-and-bathtub cleaner."

Right when I was getting up some nice momentum, the bell rang and I had to get back in line. Which was probably a good thing, because Winnie Rae was looking like she was getting ready to come at me.

I leaned back and whispered to Sarah Lynn, "How Mrs. Early gets down low to scrub those motel toilet bowls and wipe out the tubs is beyond me."

Sarah Lynn giggled and nudged me up the steps to the main hallway.

I breathed deep and waited for the school smell to creep in. I didn't feel this way anywhere else. From the first time I walked through the kindergarten doors, I'd sniffed out the pencil sharpener and the stacks of new paper and I'd felt every part of my body relax.

I sat down at my desk and took out my morning journal. My pencil hardly needed any direction. I'd had something in my head since yesterday, and my pencil was practically moving on its own.

I was thinking I might like to add a short story to my poetry collection. It could maybe give me an edge over the competition. Something a little different. A little longer.

Mrs. Rodriguez walked by and put her hand on my shoulder. "Nice job on your essay, Harper." When she smiled she had a big space between her top front teeth. Sometimes you could hear a quiet whistle coming through. "You've got a special gift for words."

She set the essay down in the corner of my desk and ran her hand over my cover sketch of Queen Eleanor of Aquitaine. "You remind me of Eleanor, you know. You're strong and creative, just like she was."

I smiled at her; I did feel like that when I was breathing in those school smells. It was a good thing I took a deep whiff that morning, because it turned out I was going to need some extra to tide me over for a while.

Chapter Four

I DIDN'T KNOW how Winnie Rae had done it with all her sniffing and wheezing, but she managed to get a good block ahead of me on the way home from school. Which meant she'd had a good block's worth of time to see everything before I did.

She spun herself around like a runway model and wasted no time in coming back to report it all to me. She stopped in front of me with her hip cocked to one side and one hand resting on the beginnings of a fat roll. "You're lucky it didn't rain today, Harper Lee Morgan," she said, "because your entire house is out on your front lawn." She had her braggy look about her, where her top lip turns up on one side.

It was easy for the mind to play tricks on a person when they were down on their luck, especially if that person was you. And my mind was thinking how maybe all that stuff piled around on the lawn belonged to somebody else—the Earlys, maybe. But my eyes were telling me different, due to the fact that Hemingway was sitting in the middle of one of the smaller piles, holding the tiny peach sweater up by one of its fluffy baby arms.

"I found it at the bottom, Harper Lee," he said. His eyes were all shiny and he looked as if he was getting ready to let loose with a good cry. "But I brushed it off real clean and I didn't let any of it touch the ground again."

"Good job, Hem." I felt my stomach get hollow and dry.

I knew that sweater belonged to Flannery, the baby that almost was. She didn't quite make it. Mama says she never even opened her eyes. I knew for a fact, if she would have opened just one of her eyes and seen Mama's beautiful smile, she might have opened the other one and hung around for a while.

"Give it here, please," I said, "before Mama sees it."

I found the red apple crate with my poems and stories in it and tucked Flannery's little sweater deep down into the side. It made my stomach feel better for a second, thinking that Flannery and my stories could take care of each other.

"You better get started, Harper Lee." Winnie Rae swept her hand in a wide arc in front of her. "You got a whole lot of mess to clean up and no house to put it in."

My eyes must have scared her, because she ran right over to her mama's lawn chair and sat herself down without another word.

Mama came around front from the back yard. She put her hand up to her mouth when she saw me, as if I was unexpected company.

"Oh, Harper," she said, "I'd hoped to have this whole thing straightened out and have everything back inside before you got home from school." She looked over her shoulder at the front door. "But everything's locked up tight as a drum."

Her eyes fell on her favorite chair, the white rocker, tilted sideways in the garden dirt, and I wished I could have gotten home first and fixed it all back for her.

Hemingway cupped his hands wide in front of him. "They got them big old padlocks on, and the windows are shut up tight."

Mama turned in a slow circle, her eyes making their way around to each and every pile. "We found it like this about an hour ago," she said. Her face was red and blotchy, with the tear tracks like she used to get in the days after Daddy first left.

Hemingway bent down and pulled a plastic dinosaur out of the top of a box. "We were coming back from cleaning Miss Oakley's kitchen, and Mama thought we took a wrong turn onto someone else's street."

"It's got to be a mistake, Mama," I said. "Look there." I pointed to a dark blue car coming up toward the house. "Mrs. Early's probably gotten someone to come take the locks off."

I wanted her to feel better, even if it was only for a second. I couldn't stand seeing her looking like all the hope had been washed out of her.

I grabbed Hem by the hand and hung back by the porch steps with Mama. I already had a plan going in my mind. The second they unhooked one of those padlocks, I was going to get me a good head start and push right past them. Then I'd refuse to come out until they put it all back right.

The lady was taking her time getting out of her car. Mainly because the driver's side looked to be so smashed up, you couldn't open the door.

Mama's eyes got dark and narrow, like when the

supermarket checker tried to give her the wrong change.

The lady scooted herself over to the other side and came out through the passenger door, but she still didn't act to be in any hurry. She leaned back in and reached over the front seat, coming out with one of those zippered pouches, which she hooked around her waist.

Hemingway nodded toward her. "Maybe that's where she keeps her lock-breaking tools."

But she didn't even walk in our general direction. She circled all the piles of cardboard boxes and scattered furniture, slowly, holding on to the zipper tab on her pouch.

Mama took a couple of steps forward and shaded her eyes with her hand. "May I help you?" she asked.

The lady stopped when she got to the pile of couch cushions by the front porch. She leaned over and pulled a toilet brush out of a box next to the bottom step and held it up, looking at Mama through the hole in the center of the brush. "Doesn't seem to be any rhyme or reason to your collection here," she said.

"What?" Mama tilted her head to the side like she was searching for the right words.

But that lady had said out loud just exactly what was going on in my own mind. The whole yard was like the clearance bin down at the Piggly Wiggly after people had been weeding through it for a few days. Whoever Mrs. Early had gotten to take all our stuff out of the house had done it as quickly as possible, by just tossing and dragging.

Hemingway's mattress and box spring were leaning up against the side of the front porch, and his dresser was over on its side, with the television from the living room sitting on top of it. There was a wide muddy grass stain on the very spot where Hem liked to curl up at night with his arms tucked under him. I couldn't stop looking at that stain, and I suddenly knew a bit about how Sarah Lynn Newhart's grandma had felt when her house burned to the ground.

Whatever could fit in boxes had been plopped into them, without any careful wrapping, or even fastening up the lids. I could see that the toilet-brush box also held Mama's best Christmas towels and the picture of my dead great-grandma.

Mama must have seen me looking, because she touched my arm real lightly and said, "Grandma spent a lot of time primping up in the bathroom in her day, so I'm sure she wouldn't mind."

I liked how Mama managed to joke a little or sound hopeful, even in a bad situation. Just like how Mr. Atticus Finch always did in *To Kill a Mockingbird*. Except for when it came to Flannery. No one was allowed to mention the baby who almost was.

Which was why I practically flew off the porch when I saw the lady bending down toward my apple crate. I knew what she was reaching for, and it wasn't my stories. But I had to make my way around a pile of kitchen chairs, and I couldn't get to her in time.

Chapter Five

THE LADY HELD UP the peach sweater and unzipped her pouch with the other hand. "How much you want for this?"

I grabbed Flannery's sweater out of her hand so quickly, I caught my fingernail across her arm. "It's not for sale!"

I held tight to the smallest hope that Mama hadn't seen what she was holding up, but as soon as I turned back around, I knew for sure that the peach color had soaked right into Mama's eyes. A tiny kitten sound came out of her mouth as she sank down on the top step of the porch.

Mama pointed across the yard to the lady's car. "You're trespassing, and you'd better get yourself off this property before I call the police." The words were strong, but Mama's voice sounded as if it was going to break at any moment.

The lady made her way to her car a lot faster than when she'd come in. She shook her head and turned toward us as she opened up the door. She pointed her chin down to her chest and looked up at us from under her eyebrows with crazy eyes, like she was delivering up a curse. "You people ain't going to sell one thing at this yard sale! No one will even set foot at this ridiculous dump!"

I wanted to go kick in the other side of that lady's car, but I saw the wobbly steps Mama was taking and I kicked away a perfectly sharp rock instead.

I went over and put my hand on Mama's shoulder and did my slow, quiet voice, like I used on Hemingway when I was reading him to sleep. "Let's rest up here on the porch, Mama, while we figure on what to do."

I smoothed out the sweater across my lap so the edge of the sleeve was touching Mama's arm. She put her arm around me and leaned down on my shoulder. Just a brush stroke of that peach fuzziness made her breathing steady right up.

It worked the same with me. Only a hint of anything Flannery made my whole body relax.

I closed my eyes and I could almost smell the baby wipes I'd brought along to the hospital to help give Flannery her first bath. I had packed those in my black patent-leather pocketbook while Daddy was helping Mama into the car in the driveway. Before we'd known Flannery wasn't going to open those eyes of hers.

You can go on in and have a look at her. Daddy had said it quietly, so Hem couldn't hear. *Just you, now, Harper Lee. Hem's too little.*

Hem wouldn't have understood about her not waking up and all.

Then Daddy had squeezed my hand and I'd gone into Mama's hospital room. Flannery was up close to Mama, in Mama's bent arm, wrapped in a peach blanket Daddy had bought for her.

It's okay to touch her. Daddy's eyes had been shiny, as if some tears were working their way out.

I had reached next to Mama and fixed the blanket so it wasn't so loose. It was chilly in that hospital room.

Mama had touched my hand, softly, but her eyes never left Flannery.

But then the nurse had given Mama a shot, and I

couldn't get myself to breathe in enough air. Then I'd started to cry, and Daddy had had to pull me away from Mama's bed.

I remembered the words that kept going through my head and inching their way out of my mouth. *What if she doesn't wake up? What if she stays asleep forever, like Flannery?*

Daddy had picked me up and held me close for what seemed like forever. And he'd helped to cool down the mad I'd suddenly felt at Hemingway. Because all Hem did was sit at the nurses' station, building a Lego garage for his Hot Wheels. Just like Flannery had never happened at all.

I LOOKED DOWN the porch steps at Hem. He was busy finding all his plastic dinosaurs and lining them up on the edge of the coffee table. "We having a yard sale, Mama?" He picked up his biggest dinosaur and squinted at the underbelly of it. "How much you think I could get for this one?"

I gave him my hush-up look and set to work searching out Mama's special book. As soon as I pulled it out of the laundry hamper, she seemed to perk right up.

I turned to her favorite chapter, which wasn't too hard. The book was creased open so good at that particular spot that when you set the book down, it automatically flopped open to that page.

It was the part where Scout finally gets to see their hermit neighbor, Boo Radley. It's where she realizes what her daddy's been trying to tell her all along. That people aren't always what they seem from the outside. You got to give them a chance and figure them out for your own self.

Hem piled the cushions back on the couch and we all sat down together in our living room in the yard.

But Mama wasn't reading like she usually did, leaned back with her eyes closed. She bent over the book in her lap, her finger tracking under the words, slowly, so Hem and me could let the story sink into our bones.

Hemingway hummed quietly to himself and held his dinosaurs so they made long shadows on the grass.

I nudged Mama softly with my shoulder. "That word is 'embarrassment,' Mama. Scout was embarrassed, not excited."

She nodded and hugged my arm. "I must've just looked wrong." The tops of her cheeks got all pink and blotchy, and she handed the book to me. "You read, Harper," she said. "I can't think right."

I took the book from her. Lately, she'd been having me read more. I'd noticed she read better with the lights out when we were going to bed at night. She tended to mix up the words here and there when she did it the other way.

I smoothed my hand over the page and took up where she left off. But after a couple of pages, I could tell Mama wasn't paying much attention. Her eyes kept traveling over the piles on our lawn.

Finally, she tapped her pointer finger on the cover of the book and pushed herself up off the couch. "We need to be good thinkers and problem solvers like Mr. Atticus Finch, and get this mess cleaned up before it gets dark on us. We'll find what we need for tonight and put it in the car."

Mr. Atticus Finch pretty much always knew what was what.

Mama looked at the light brown sedan parked up next to the house, and I thought how all my clothes would smell like old lady. We had gotten that car all the way from Mississippi when my grandma died. *That old lady never gave me the time of day,* Mama had told Daddy when we were driving him to the bus station. *She never even laid eyes on my children, and now we're paying more than the cost of that decrepit car for you to go on out and get it.*

Hem and I had poked around in Daddy's mama's car for a couple of days when Daddy got back, hoping we could sniff out some gold or diamonds or something she might have hidden in there, but all we smelled was stale old lady. Kind of a mixture of fried onions and a closet that hadn't been aired out in a while. And that smell held on, too. Every time I took even a little ride in that car, I could smell it on me for a good two hours after.

I pointed at a box of kitchen bowls with some toilet-tissue rolls spilling over the top. "I say we try to organize by room." I picked up a toilet-tissue roll and tucked it under my arm. "Like this here." I tilted the box so Hem could see. "It's mostly kitchen bowls. So we just ignore the toilet paper and put the whole box in the kitchen section."

"That's a good idea, Harper Lee." Mama nudged one of Hem's dresser drawers with her toe. "Then we can figure out what to take with us tonight."

"We can't get all this in the car, can we?" I imagined my bed and the big mirror from Mama's vanity balanced on the top of Daddy's mama's car. If only Daddy hadn't driven away in the big white pickup last year, we might have had something to work with.

Mama's eyes went from the car to the yard, and she shook her head. Her eyebrows wrinkled up tight, like they did when she was paging through the back of her checkbook. "I haven't yet thought what to do with it all. I guess we'll just have to get what we can for tonight and come back tomorrow."

I wanted to ask her where we were going to come back from, but she had that closed-up look on her face, like she got when she was done with people bothering her for the day.

Hem helped for a while, until he found a box with food from the kitchen and settled down on the couch with it.

Mama looked over from the bathroom pile. "He's not nibbling on any raw meat or anything from the fridge, is he, Harper Lee? I had a chicken defrosting before I left this morning."

I squinted my eyes up at him. "Naw, it looks like a couple of graham crackers is all."

I'd started to go over and get a better look at what he was gnawing on when I caught sight of something over my right shoulder, and it was stinking like Winnie Rae.

"You just go on back where you came from, Winnie Rae Early." I held up a long box of fireplace matches, like I might be getting ready to fling them at her.

"And that's just like you, isn't it, Harper?" Winnie Rae stood next to a Radio Flyer wagon. She peeled at flecks of black paint along the handle. "Here I come offering up my assistance, and you're your mean old self. My mama pointed out to me just today that you can have a bite like a venomous viper snake."

Anyone in her right mind knew that Winnie Rae Early never offered up anything just for the sake of niceness. There was a price of some sort rolling around in that Radio Flyer of hers. There always was.

"Mrs. Morgan." She gave up on me and turned her handle toward Mama. "We got a nice old shed out to the side of the house. Mama said you could maybe use our big rolling cart with the fold-down ramp and put some of your stuff out there. She said you could store some of your things that aren't too heavy out in the camper."

I noticed no one offered to let us stay out in that camper. Just a few things that didn't weigh too much. I guessed that left Mrs. Early out of the camping trailer, which meant she was one less person trying to rifle through our personal belongings.

But when I thought about it that way, it made it a whole lot easier to sort and pack things away. Big things like furniture went into the shed, things I couldn't bear to have come in contact with anything Early went into the car, and everything that I didn't care much about, or could have the Early washed off of, went into the camper up next to their house.

"Oh, yeah." Winnie Rae pointed at the front porch behind us. "Mama said to make sure no one tries to put anything back up on the porch. She doesn't want Grandma's house looking like some junky old eyesore from the road."

She always talked about her grandmother as if she was getting ready to come walking across the yard at any time and take our home back. But we all knew her grandmother hadn't been doing any walking for quite some time now. She'd been long dead, since way before Winnie Rae was even born.

I was thinking on all sorts of mean things I could say in return, but I noticed that as Winnie Rae was taking herself home across the grass, she looked back with her eye on my green dresser with the blue flower decals.

And I erased that coveting thought right out of her mind with a good evil eye to the middle of her forehead.

When we'd finally packed ourselves into the car, I sat on top of Mama's best antique lace towels from her mama and held tightly to Hemingway, so he wouldn't slide off the three-legged stool that Mama's daddy had built when he was sixteen years old.

I could see Winnie Rae to the side of her shed. The sunlight was almost completely gone for the day, but I could still see the outline of her, crouched like a chubby little animal, watching us.

I knew Winnie Rae to keep her bicycle and her antique-doll collection out in that shed, and I wanted Mama to drive right through the closest wall and see how Winnie Rae liked seeing her own things spilling around in the dirt.

Hemingway had one eye on the car window to the side of him. He wasn't used to riding up that high, and with every little turn of the steering wheel, his hand squeezed my arm, as if he was worried he was going to crash on through the glass.

"Sit tight, now." Mama put her right hand around me, her elbow touching the back of the seat where I'd set out Flannery's little peach sweater.

I looked up in Mama's rearview mirror, but the

house was blocked by all of our piles. I wondered if Daddy'd had anything blocking his way when he left in his pickup. But then I remembered to ignore my thoughts of him, and I made my mind toss them in the pile beside our old house where we'd left what was broken or used up.

Chapter Six

A MOTOR HOTEL sounds downright fancy on a big lit-up sign, but I knew the Knotty Pine Deluxe Motor Hotel to be where Mrs. Ione Early worked, and there was nothing fancy about it.

I ran the tips of my fingers up and down the slick wood paneling on the walls. Someone had scratched *Leona* in perfect cursive above one of the beds. Hemingway took a running start from the door and dived onto the first bed. He sat up and took a couple of handfuls of the rusty orange bedspread and got himself a good bounce going.

Mama looked at him, but I could tell she was too tired to get him to stop. "Keep an eye on your brother, Harper," she said. "I need to bring some things in from the car."

I flipped on the overhead light, and it made a spidery orange glow in the middle of the ceiling.

Hemingway grabbed on to the tan wooden headboard and pulled himself up on his knees. "I love horses. They're almost as fast as dinosaurs." He pressed his nose up against the painting on the wall above the bed and bounced his knees on the pillow. "These horses feel like your Christmas dress."

"It's velvet," I said. "The artist painted right on the velvet."

He leaned back a little and got a better bounce going.

"Watch yourself, Hemingway." I put my hand out next to the orange ceramic lamp. The base of the lamp looked like the bumpy round squash Mama bought for her special casserole around Thanksgiving time. "There's breakable stuff in here."

Mama carried in a cardboard box and set it down against the wall across from the foot of Hem's bed. She held her arms out wide and walked in a straight line along the side wall. "We can stack quite a few things here against the wall, but we need to be sure to leave a walkway."

I saw the pointy ear of my favorite stuffed animal

sticking out of the top of the box. My gray cat had sat on my pillow since I had learned to make my own bed. But it looked so out of place on the motel bedspread, and I wished I was back in my own bed, looking at the green crayon letters Hemingway had drawn on my light blue walls.

I stood with my back to the side of the wide front window and rested my hand on a little round table. I pointed to my left. "We should leave this clear, too. So we can get into the bathroom."

The door to the bathroom hung from the top of the doorframe and folded up to one side when you opened it, like an accordion fan.

Hemingway followed me inside.

"Looks like Mrs. Early missed a few spots on this one." I moved a tiny shampoo bottle and sat on the edge of the tub. I leaned forward onto the side of the sink next to me and rested my chin on my arms. I tried not to think of anything Early touching the tub that I was going to be using.

Hem put down the lid on the toilet on the other side of the sink and made himself comfortable. "Maybe that baby got in the way." He arched his back and pushed his stomach out hard.

"Hush, now, you two," Mama said. She held her

hand to the side of her mouth, as if she was trying not to smile. "She was nice enough to give us these two-for-one coupons, and heaven knows we can use all the help we can get."

A plastic tray on the back of the toilet held four glasses and an empty plastic ice bucket, made to look like it was brown wood. I grabbed one of the drinking glasses and picked at a loose end of the cellophane, unwrapping the glass from its crinkly plastic cocoon.

"What's it say on the glass there, Harper Lee?" Hem tilted his head to the side and looked to be trying to get his mouth around the sounds of the letters on the side of the glass.

I held it up to the light and made out the faded green letters. "Says here Knotty Pine Luxury Cabins." I turned on the faucet and waited for the water to get cold. "These don't seem like cabins to me." I filled up my glass and took a long drink. "I always thought cabins to be standing alone in some trees all by themselves." I listened to the toilet flush on the other side of our bathroom wall.

"These rooms are stuck together tight." Hem reached back and flushed the toilet, as if he was trying to answer the people next door. "Anyway, I thought this was the Knotty Pine Deluxe Motor Hotel." He said "de-luxe" as if it was two separate words.

"People can make anything fancy with the right words," I said. "Hand me my blue notebook, would you, Hem?"

I sat back down on the edge of the tub and leaned forward onto the sink. Maybe if I thought about my stories or poems it would seem more like home.

I could see Mama through the doorway, sitting cross-legged on one of the double beds. She had a white tablet on her lap, and she looked to be doing some figuring of her own.

Hem tossed me my notebook and sat down next to Mama with his crayons. "Can we still have school at home if this isn't my real home?"

Mama tilted her head but kept her eyes on her tablet, like she wasn't really listening.

"Mama," I said, "you ought to think on letting Hemingway go to the regular old kindergarten."

She turned the tablet over on her lap and looked across at me. "You know that wouldn't work out, Harper Lee. Kindergarten's only half a day. I can't be leaving work to take him back and forth."

I stood in the doorway. "He could walk home on

his own and take care of himself for a few hours, Mama. Just until I get home."

She took a deep breath. "One of these days, things will be different. When I get you and Hem all the way through school, maybe I can take my own self back to school." She sat up against the headboard. "My mother always did want me to finish high school."

She made her voice all slow, and cut her words off like she did when she was imitating her mama's Louisiana talk. *"Girl that reads and makes up stories as much as you, ought to finish up her school."*

I finished the story for her like I always did. "But she was sick and you had to take care of her. You spent your high school taking care of your brothers and sisters."

She nodded. "No way my father knew how to take care of a sick wife and a whole ream of children. He could barely take care of himself."

I thought about how I'd feel if I was trying to do my homework or write a poem and I had that ream of brothers and sisters climbing all over me.

Then I thought of something she'd never really talked about. "Who took care of that ream of children after my daddy came and rescued you?"

She looked out the window as if she was searching out someone way far off. "My mama died right before your daddy started coming around. The day after the funeral, my father shipped all six of those kids off deeper down into the Louisiana bayou to live with my mama's sisters."

I looked over at Hem. I sure wouldn't want him shipped off anywhere.

"It's been a very long day, Harper." Mama flopped back on the bed and covered her face with her arms. "I can't talk about all this right now."

And even though I didn't think she meant to, she fell asleep right then and there.

I tucked my notebook under my arm and rinsed out my Knotty Pine Luxury Cabins water glass. "Come here, Hem." I picked up the shampoo bottle. "Your hair could use a good washing."

I ran warm water into the tub and tipped out some of the shampoo under the spout.

I helped him get his shirt over his head and put my arm out to steady him as he climbed into the tub.

"Make lots of bubbles, Harper Lee. I like lots of bubbles." He scooted to the back of the tub. He'd been afraid of the drain for as long as I could remember. He wouldn't even put his toes near it.

"I know, Hem." I picked up the ice bucket and dipped it into the bath water. "Now tip your head down and close your eyes."

I pushed the faucet off with my elbow and poured the sudsy water over his brown curls. The water straightened them out against his neck in long waves, just like mine. He favored me in the eyes, too. Green and wide and sad in the deep-down parts. They had rivers and roads jutting out from the centers, where everything had sunk itself in. The roads of worry were the Mama part of him.

I rubbed the washcloth at his neck and he twisted away from me. "Not so hard, Harper Lee."

"You got a ring of dirt around your neck a thumb wide, Hem." I dabbed under his chin. "You don't want people thinking there's no one taking care of you." I tilted his chin up and put the washcloth in his hand. "You do it, then." I sat on the edge of the tub and waited. Every bit of the mixed-up anger and sadness from the day was creeping into my arms and legs, all of a sudden like, and I knew I could fall asleep without trying, just like Mama. I tried to push aside the picture in my mind of the Earlys, marching through our house and rifling through our personal things.

"Okay. Clean enough." I pulled Hem out of the tub and wrapped him in a long towel. "If you get your teeth brushed right now, we'll still have time to read a quick story."

I tossed him one of Mama's working T-shirts. It was perfect for sleeping. All soft and stretchy from being so worn. But he set it down and pulled his usual pajamas out of his pillowcase—a sleeveless cotton undershirt of Daddy's. I was kind of hoping it had gotten lost in the front-yard mess. Every time I laid eyes on it, I tried to think of it as Hemingway's. But that low, whiskey voice always seemed to pour out of one of the side seams and aim itself at my blue writing notebook.

I opened my notebook and took the light blue paper from the pocket inside the front cover.

This year, no whiskey-soaked pen would get in the way of my entry form.

I hugged my notebook. This year's collection was shaping up to be the best bunch of poems I'd ever written. And I'd even be throwing in a short story at the end, to show those judges I meant business.

Chapter Seven

"WAKE UP, HARPER LEE. I need you to listen to me for a minute." It was Mama's voice, all right, but it was hard to make out the shape of Mama, because my eyes still thought it was the middle of the night.

And sure enough, when I rolled over to face the red electric numbers on the Knotty Pine alarm clock, I could see it was only two minutes past three o'clock. "You okay, Mama?" I sat up on my elbows. "You sick or something?"

"No, Harper, I'm fine." She pushed a piece of hair to the side of my face. "I need you to do me a favor, is all."

Hem kicked me in his sleep, and I gave his legs a good push so they were hanging partway off the other side of the bed. I could smell coffee from the little drip machine on top of the short box refrigerator next to the door.

"I need you to take care of Hemingway for me today." She sat down on my side of the bed and buttoned the top button on her fisherman's knit sweater.

"Can't you take him with you like usual?" I yanked a couple of feet of blanket over to my side.

She shook her head. "I have to go right now. I'm sorry I didn't tell you last night, but I fell dead asleep before I got to it. Girl that opens the Laundromat has been getting there late for the past couple of weeks. Word has it she didn't even show yesterday. So I'm going to go down there and see if I can't pick up the extra job."

I looked over at Hemingway. "It's hard to get ready for school with him underfoot."

I guess it was right then and there that I knew something was up. The air between Mama and me seemed to get stuffier all of a sudden, and she wouldn't look at me.

"Well, that's just it, Harper Lee." Her eyes were darting all over the place, like Hem's did when he was doing something he knew was wrong. "I have to go right over to my housecleaning job after the Laundromat. I'll be late if I come back here to get Hem." She finally looked me in the eye. "You know I wouldn't ask this of you if I didn't absolutely have to."

Now it was me that wouldn't look at her straight-on.

"Listen, Harper. I don't have time to be driving you to school today, anyway."

"I don't need you to drive me, Mama." I knew I was whining like Hem now, but I couldn't help myself. "I'll just stand up on the main road and flag down a school bus."

But she was already partway through the door. "Put on the chain lock when I leave."

I got up to go to the door, and she turned and looked back at me. "For heaven's sakes. Give me a break here, Harper. It's only one day. And this is for all of us."

I nodded. "All right." I said it, but nothing really was right at all.

She reached out and put her hand on my cheek. It was cool against my warm face, and it always made me feel better when she did that.

"I'm not sure how long I'll be," she said. "I might have to work into the evening. There's some bologna and cheese in the little fridge, and half a loaf of bread on the table." Then she blew me a kiss and pulled the door shut behind her.

I pulled the covers back up and tried to go back to

sleep, but my mind wouldn't let me. Looking at Hemingway all sprawled out and sleeping so nicely caused the angry worry to simmer up again. It was slow in coming, and it made my muscles go stiff and tight. I was thinking for a quick second that I might not even like Hem, but I knew that was only the Daddy part of me coming out. My teacher said people are born with a little something from both parents. I was always hoping my Mama part would shine through.

I wanted to run after Mama and tell her I wouldn't do it. I had waited a whole year for that poetry contest to come around again, and I couldn't be staying home for Hemingway, even for one day. I wanted to do it, but my legs stayed put, because Mama was long gone by then.

The motel VACANCY sign outside the window was looking like Winnie Rae Early when she was trying to get into someone's business, flashing and moving all around in bursts of speed. When Mama had closed the door, the bottom edge of the curtain had blown up on the windowsill, and the sign was flashing red neon bursts on the top of my poetry notebook.

There was less than a week until the contest and I hadn't even gotten started with the proofreading. Teachers and parents had to proofread every poem and story, not just for spelling errors and such, but because of Worley Buckley's use of profanity in the contest two years ago. He had gotten up to the microphone to read his first piece, and no one could get to him fast enough.

It was about his grandma, which seemed like a nice, safe subject, so no one saw it coming. I could remember almost word for word how it started:

My grandma, she lived all alone.
She had company, but now she has none.
She took meals with her talking dog, Bart,
but her cooking made the two of them fart.
He'd sniff and he'd smell,
Then he'd say, "What the—"

Worley Buckley got a good solid handful of dirty words out before the vice-principal hauled him, by the hood of his sweatshirt, out the side door of the auditorium.

I sat down at the round table by the window with my notebook and thought on what to write. Hem breathed out a choppy snore and broke my concentration.

And that's when I saw her out of the corner of my eye. She stood in the middle of the parking lot outside. The "C" in the middle of the sign flashed orangey red on the side of her face and her whole pink stocking cap seemed to light up.

She looked old, but not wobbly grandma old. She had a wheelchair, but she didn't sit and ride. She stood and pushed. And when it came down to it, she wouldn't have had any room to sit, even if she'd wanted to. The seat was piled high with grocery bags, only they didn't seem to be filled with food of any sort. In fact, I could see a chair leg poking out of the top of one of them.

She was wearing a suit. A man's business suit, like the kind the school principal wore. And she had pajamas on over the top, and some bedroom slippers to go with it all.

She must've known how hard I was looking, because she turned that wheelchair clean around and pushed her gray hair to the sides of her face as if to get a better look going. She didn't get any closer to my window. She stayed under that flashing VACANCY sign and stared. She held her eyes there for a good long while before she slowly turned and wheeled off across the parking lot, as if she was starting out fresh with another day.

The thing is, a person might think getting stared down like that would be downright creepy. But not from this old lady. I didn't know what it was, but looking at her got my brain going every which way, thinking about this and that, and it put me in the right mind for some good poetry writing.

Soon as I got the title in my head, all the rest of the words followed right after it.

Also Known As Harper

by Harper Lee Morgan

I have been Harper Lee Morgan
Mostly all of my life.
The way I figure
That name has soaked itself into my bones.
Lately, though,
I've been figuring on something different.
Something without the Daddy part hooked on.
Being just plain Harper Lee
Might help my brother know
It's time to come in from that long wait on the porch.
Being just plain Harper Lee
Might help my mama know
It's not her fault Flannery never opened her eyes.
It'd be nice to start out fresh
Without the ragged part of me
Tagging along behind.

Chapter Eight

HEMINGWAY SAT SIDEWAYS in the doorway of the motel room, with one foot in and one foot out. "You having school at home today, too, Harper Lee?" He wore the red T-shirt and grubby jeans he'd had on yesterday, but I had too much on my mind to bother him about it.

"I guess so." I was trying not to think about what I was missing. Mrs. Rodriguez had said just yesterday that a teacher could only do so much, and if we didn't hand in our poems to her soon, she wouldn't have enough time to proofread them all. We'd be plain out of luck.

"What we going to start on first?" He licked at a crumbly corner of his graham cracker.

Watching him talk with the light brown cakey stuff in the corners of his mouth usually didn't bother me one bit. But today it was making me cranky mad. "You'd better close that door, Hemingway, or we're going to be getting some giant bugs in here." I said that last part on purpose, because I was still feeling pretty ugly, and I knew how much he hated june bugs and cockroaches and such.

He slammed that door so fast, he practically took his own toe off in the process. "She was out there again."

"Who?" I ran my hand over the long bumps of rust corduroy on the bedspread.

He opened the little square refrigerator and took out a package of cheese. "The old lady." He smelled a square of cheese and licked the clear cellophane on the outside. "She was wheeling around the parking lot when we got here. Didn't you see her?"

I shook my head. "Not when we first got here."

"Then I saw her again last night." He slowly peeled back the wrapper on the cheese. "She was by our window when I got up to go to the bathroom."

So he'd seen her, too. I hoped he wasn't planning on trying to talk to her. I wanted to be the one to talk to her, but I was picking and choosing my words. I wanted to ask her about what she was carrying around in that wheelchair, but she was looking like a person that kept things private. I'd have to think real careful on what I was going to say.

Hemingway took a big bite of his cheese and pointed at a bottom corner of the window. "That kid needs to wipe his nose."

A grubby face about the size of Hemingway's was pressed up against the glass. Hands were cupped around the eyes as if he was trying to see inside our room better.

I put on my Mama face and waved the kid away, but he didn't budge. He was mouthing something I couldn't quite make out.

Hem must have understood some of it, because, the next thing I knew, he had opened the door and was waving the kid inside.

"I can't play with you until you wipe your nose." Hemingway handed the kid the box of tissues from the little table.

The kid shrugged and reached for a tissue. "Okay." He blew his nose real hard, and when he wiped away a good portion of the dirt on the bottom half of his face, I could see he had a nice little smile. The kind of smile that made you like him, even if you hadn't planned on it.

Smack-dab in the middle of his shirt was a stick-on

name tag with RANDALL KELLEY written in thick red marker. The sides were all peeled up, and it looked to be getting ready to come off.

It wasn't until he sat himself down at our table and lit into our box of graham crackers that I noticed the girl that had stepped in behind him. She seemed to be my age around about the face, but I knew her mama would never be needing to take up any of her hems. We probably weighed near about the same, but she had a good solid foot on me.

"Hey," I said.

There was something friendly and kind about the way her eyes crinkled up when she smiled, and she looked to be the sort of person you could trust. The sort of person that would appreciate a good poem.

"She doesn't talk." Randall had helped himself to the graham-cracker box, and he was pulling at the waxy flap of a new package. "Her name's Lorraine."

"Hey, Lorraine." I tried to make my eyes look crinkly and friendly. "I'm Harper Lee." I pointed behind me. "Hemingway. But we usually call him Hem." I felt my face get all hot when I realized what I'd just said. If Lorraine didn't talk, she wouldn't be calling Hemingway much of anything.

"How come she doesn't talk?" Hemingway grabbed the graham-cracker package back.

Randall shrugged. "She's not retarded or anything. Mama says she's just choosing her words carefully. Some people don't run off at the mouth at the drop of a hat."

I thought about Winnie Rae Early and I nodded. It might be nice to be around someone who was more careful with her words.

"She used to talk." Randall tilted his head up and to the side like he was remembering. "But one day, a year ago, she just stopped."

I looked at Lorraine, but her eyes had found the cover of my poetry notebook as if Randall wasn't right then talking about her personal business. Her fingers were following the swirly design I'd made with my purple marking pen.

Hem pointed at a corner of Randall's name tag. "All the sticky's gone off of it. Might as well just throw it away."

He shook his head. "Can't. Mama will get mad." He tried to smooth a corner back down with his thumb. "She puts them on everything. She's hoping it will make Lorraine find her words."

Lorraine didn't seem as if she had lost much of

anything. From the way she looked about the eyes, I was without a doubt sure that she had plenty of words moving around inside her head.

She lifted the corner on the cover of my poetry notebook and leaned toward me with her eyebrows raised high.

I nodded. "Sure, go right ahead." I liked to watch what people did when they read my poems, how their shoulders and their eyes moved. I wanted to know if they felt the same way when they read them as I did when I was writing the words.

She turned the pages slowly until she got to the poem I wrote last August. Back when Mama took me school shopping at the St. Vincent de Paul Thrift Store.

I watched Lorraine's eyes move across the page and I read the words in my mind.

Some people like things shiny and crisp
But I tend to like the things with the scraped up edges.
That way I can tell other people have liked them too.
They've torn them and spilled on them
Or broken off a corner or two
As they went about the important business
Of their day.

Something smooth and straight and new
Has an emptiness about it
Because it hasn't been important
To anyone yet.

Lorraine looked up at me and smoothed down her skirt that used to be bright purple. She smiled part of a smile, and I knew she was going to be my friend.

Chapter Nine

I WATCHED RANDALL as he sat down on the end of the bed and opened Hemingway's handwriting book. As soon as he started moving in that direction, I knew what would happen next.

Sure enough, Hemingway pulled it quickly out of his hands. He was real private about his letters, especially his "b"s, which he sometimes got mixed up with his "d"s and "p"s. "What grade you in?" Hem asked him.

Randall wrinkled his nose. "I guess you could say I'm in the second grade." He glanced at Lorraine. "But I never actually finished the first grade and we didn't ever get a chance to sign me up for school here." His eyes lit on Hem's handwriting book. "Mama said we were taking our summer vacation early last year, because we're going up north. There's a special doctor up there that's going to help Lorraine find her words."

Lorraine's hands got shaky right down to the fingertips when he said that, and her eyebrows narrowed and scrunched together as if Randall's words made her nervous and upset, all at the same time.

Hem didn't seem to notice one little bit. His shoulders got droopy when Randall mentioned the part about going up north, as if they'd been best friends for years or something.

"So you'll be moving on in the morning, I s'pose," Hem said.

But Randall sat back against the radiator, looking like he wasn't in any hurry at all. "We ran out of money a while back." He put his hands out wide. "Mama said we were going to hang around here for a while."

Hem looked toward the window. "Your mama outside?"

Randall shook his head. "She's off running her errands." He kicked against the front of the tan metal radiator with his heel. "We're not going anywhere just yet. She said we're sitting tight here for a bit. Until she can think on what to do."

"Just like us!" Hem acted as if waiting on money was something fun and exciting.

But I knew the truth, and I could tell by the sad worry in Lorraine's hands that she knew it, too.

She folded and unfolded her hands in front of her, as if she couldn't find the proper place for them.

I looked at Flannery's sweater, laid out on top of the three-legged stool. Everything we'd hauled with us was stacked up against the side wall. At our house, I'd never had to think about what to do with anything. Everything had a closet or a drawer.

Lorraine opened the door and leaned out, shading her eyes with her hand. She turned to Randall and motioned him toward the door with her other hand.

"Is it our turn?" Randall stuffed another graham cracker into his pocket and headed for the door.

Lorraine turned to me with her crinkly-eye smile and waved.

"Hold on." Randall skipped back toward our bathroom.

He came out with a bar of soap and one of the little white shampoo bottles. "Can I have these?" He held them up carefully, as if they were fragile dishes. "I'll bring back the extra."

I looked at the tiny dirt streaks about the sides of his face. Maybe Mrs. Early was getting skimpy with the shampoo when she scrubbed out the tub in their motel room. "Wait a second." I reached behind the chair for my soda-cracker box, where I kept the sunflower toilet water and fancy hair conditioner I'd gotten on my last birthday. I held them out to Lorraine. "Here. Use what you need and give the rest back later."

She turned the bottles to see the labels and put her hand to the side of her face. Curling a dark brown piece of hair around her finger, she smiled at me. It was the kind that started out slow and stayed on her face for a while.

After they left, I couldn't get Hem to focus on his letters. His attention kept moving to the window. "Let's go see if they can play," he said. "They should be done washing up by now."

Finally, I gave up and followed Hem out the door and down the walkway. He stopped at the very end, in front of Room 12. "This is where they live. I saw them go in here."

I could hear water running inside. "I'm not sure they're finished washing up."

Right as Hem was raising his arm up to knock, the door swung open. A tall, skinny woman with a towel on her head and a baby on her hip held the door open with her foot and smiled at us. "Go on in," she said. "We're almost finished."

I figured her to be Lorraine and Randall's mother. But before I could think on it much more, I got pushed to the side by a pointy elbow, and Hem was knocked to the ground beside me.

The pointy elbows belonged to a girl with tangled black hair that hung down practically to her behind. When she stood in front of me, we were level, eye to eye, and her two front teeth tilted up and out as if they were reaching toward me, getting ready to spear me. Those elbows of hers reminded me straight-away of Winnie Rae Early's. They looked as if they could poke themselves right through into someone's business.

She had a dirty green towel draped around her neck that had a gas-station bathroom smell to it. She must have noticed me sniffing, because she reared up her skinny chest and arched her back to try to stick it out farther, acting all big and smart, like Winnie Rae enjoyed doing. "Unh-uh," she said. "You think you're going to cut in front of me, you two got another think coming!"

Hem's eyes were round and shiny, as if he hadn't quite decided if he was going to cry or not.

I put my hand out and pulled him to his feet.

Pointy Elbows jabbed her finger in the air over Hem's head. "You make an appointment, like everyone else."

I dusted off Hem's backside. "That better not be Randall and Lorraine's sister."

She ignored me and stepped inside the motel room, slamming the door.

I looked over Hem's head to where she'd pointed, and there stood the woman with the wheelchair. Her stocking cap was gone, and her wiry gray hair spun away from her head in tight swirls. The suit jacket she'd been wearing before was hanging from one of the handles of the wheelchair, and she rested her hand against the other handle, as if she was afraid of someone taking off with it.

She looked at me dead in the eye, like she knew me, and motioned for me to come over.

Chapter Ten

I HAD HALFWAY decided I wasn't going anywhere near that woman, but Hem was across the parking lot before I could even try to stop him. He chatted with the wheelchair lady like she was the supermarket checkout girl that used to give him sugar cookies.

"What you got in that wheelchair?" Hem pointed at the big side wheel with his toe.

The lady shrugged. "A little of this. And a little of that."

"Anyone ever hurt their leg and have to ride in it?" Hem leaned all his weight to one side as if he might be getting ready to have one of his injuries.

She shook her head and straightened her stocking cap. "Not lately."

There was a chilly bite to the air, but my forehead was sweating. I bounced a little in my sneakers, in case I might have to spring into action and grab Hem out of the wheelchair lady's clutches. But the honest truth was, she didn't seem to be going anywhere very fast in her brown step-in bedroom slippers. I moved up behind Hemingway and touched his shoulder, and I tried not to look the lady in the face.

Randall came around the corner from the back of the motel and galloped over. "Hey, Dorothy." He picked up a clipboard that hung from a string at the back of the lady's wheelchair and handed it to Lorraine. She scribbled something on it and gave it back to the lady.

Randall didn't look to be anywhere near afraid of that wheelchair lady. He was standing right up next to her, as if he talked to her all the time.

I could see that Lorraine wasn't afraid of Dorothy, either. In fact, she had her eyes fixed on Dorothy like I think I might've looked at my grandma, if I'd ever had the chance to meet her.

"Mama says we should ask you if you have more openings toward the end of the week, on account of we might be using the pool this week," Randall said to Dorothy.

I really wanted to see what was on that clipboard. I couldn't think what Lorraine might be signing them up for. But Dorothy let the clipboard dangle from the handle of the wheelchair. It got to twirling, and I couldn't get my eyes around it.

Lorraine was trying to finger-comb her wet hair, and Dorothy rooted around in a green knapsack and pulled out a bright-yellow comb. She motioned for Lorraine to turn around and slowly worked at a tangled spot of hair at the back of Lorraine's neck. She patted Lorraine's head softly as she smoothed the snarl out. "Tell your mother I might have to switch some people around, but I'll see what I can do."

Lorraine smiled up into Dorothy's face, and when I finally peeked at her face myself, I could see what Lorraine was smiling about.

Dorothy's cheeks didn't have any makeup on them, but they were the color of Flannery's sweater. The skin around her eyes had lines traveling every which way. Her eyes themselves didn't have one inch of mean, but they looked like they knew things. Things about people. Maybe things that people didn't know about their own selves.

When I stepped in closer, I could smell my sunflower toilet water. Lorraine must've heard me sniffing, because she reached into a motel laundry bag and handed me my special conditioner and toilet water.

I smiled at her. "Your hair looks pretty," I said. "And the smell floats around you real nicely."

"Mama said you can come by and go swimming, if you want." Randall had a fresh name tag stuck across his shirt.

I looked around close by and off in the distance, but I didn't see a hint of a swimming pool or even a bit of lake or river.

I hadn't seen one when we'd driven in, either. And Winnie Rae had never mentioned a pool when she bragged about her mama working here, which was plain out of character for her. She was always bragging on having one thing or another, and the way she talked about it, you would've thought they owned the motel or something. Just because you clean it doesn't mean you own it.

"It's not hot yet," Hem said. "Usually, we wait until it's time to go barefoot before we go through the sprinkler or anything."

"If you're going to go, you got to go now." Randall smoothed at a corner of his name tag. "You got to go after the first rains. You wait too long, it'll be too dirty."

Dorothy looked at me and nodded. She set her clipboard on top of the pile in her wheelchair and shuffled off in her bedroom slippers. When her eyes had looked down into mine, I could have sworn she was reading one of my poems I'd been working on in my head. And she'd stared at my right hand. My writing hand.

Then it was almost as if Dorothy had shifted some words around in my head, changing my poem for me. I wanted to get back to my notebook, right away, but Hem had his feet firmly planted in the ground by Randall, and from the sounds of it, he was dead set on going swimming in April.

"I don't even know where to look for your bathing suit," I told him. "It's probably back in Winnie Rae Early's camping trailer."

"He doesn't need a suit," Randall said. "He can wear what he's got on. That's what I'm doing." He tugged at the bottom of his blue-striped T-shirt and wiped his palms on the front of his jeans.

I looked at Lorraine, but she shrugged. Seemed Randall was like Hem. Once he got an idea in his head, there was no talking him out of it.

I breathed out a loud puff of air. "Wait here, then," I said. I ran back to the room for my notebook and a towel. I wasn't so sure Mama would be happy about Hem going for a swim, but I wasn't going to worry about that right then. I had enough on my mind.

I wrapped two towels around my neck, and Hem and me followed Lorraine and Randall around the corner of the end unit.

When we got out back, I didn't even see a kiddie pool. It was as if the area was long ago forgotten.

Whoever swept and picked up out front, had completely left out the area right behind the motel. We had to step carefully back there, because most of what I saw was batches of crumbled-up concrete with bits and pieces of tall grass poking through.

I kicked aside the torn scraps of a potato-chip bag and I caught a heavy smell in the air, like a stuffy closet.

"Let's swing!" Hem galloped ahead to an old red swing set.

Even before we got there, I could see that the swing parts of it were pretty much gone. Part of one hung by a long single chain. There was a good space for the other swing, but all that was left were two short chains hanging down from the bar.

Hem grabbed on tight to the long chain and tried to hoist himself up.

I wrapped my arms around his belly and pulled

him back. "You can let go of that right now," I said. "The whole rusty thing is liable to topple back onto you."

Hem looked to be tightening his grip, but Randall shook his head. "I'm not allowed on it, either."

Behind the swing set the chipped-up concrete crumbled into dark, wet dirt, and a wide cluster of fir trees rose up in the short clumps of weeds.

"Watch out for the sticker bushes." Randall rubbed at a long scratch on his arm as we followed Lorraine down a narrow dirt path between the trees.

"So where's the pool?" I asked. The trees were getting thicker the farther we went, and I couldn't figure out why the pool was so far from the motel.

"We're 'bout there," Randall said.

If you didn't know it was there, you could easily have missed the tunneled-out passageway off to the left in the blackberry bushes.

"Duck your head and tuck in your arms," Randall called back to us. "Dorothy's got to get in here with her hedge clippers now that winter's over."

I brought my arms in close to my sides and ducked through the short, stickery passageway. And there it was. A perfect square of a pool that still had a cracked concrete border around it. Three green lawn chairs that looked to be almost new were scooted up to the edge at the far end.

I could see right off we were the first ones there, and the water in the pool was as still as could be, without one single ripple.

"No diving," Randall said. "It's not deep enough yet. We got to wait for a few more rains."

The pool was about halfway full with what I figured to be rainwater and maybe some melted snow from the past winter. Clumps of dirt made polka dots throughout the water. The inside edges of the pool were blue-green concrete that had worn itself off in white blotches, so that it looked like it had been sponge-painted.

I pulled my sweatshirt tighter around me. I was shivering, and I hadn't even stuck a toe in the water.

Lorraine smiled at me, as if she knew what I was thinking, and kicked off her blue sneakers.

"It's fine, once you get in." Randall peeled off his socks.

The pool was surrounded by a fence of tall, thick sticker bushes. And when I looked off above them real hard, I could see what I thought were white flags fluttering in the distance.

I pointed toward the flags. "Is that a carnival over

there?" I thought about how nice it would be to have a Ferris wheel or even a merry-go-round nearby.

Randall followed my finger with his eyes and shook his head. "That's the old drive-in."

I wanted to head right over there, but I knew those things didn't usually start up until after dark. You couldn't see the movie screen until the daylight was completely gone.

I turned back toward the pool and thought about taking off my shoes.

Lorraine was the first one in. She didn't jump off the edge like I usually did, but she stepped backward down a broken ladder into the side of the pool. Randall and Hemingway followed right after her.

Randall treaded water, his hands moving the water like the inside of a washing machine. "Do like this," he said. "It makes the dirt settle down to the bottom." He pushed aside the top of a yellow plastic truck.

"Doesn't someone come around and clean it, like they do at the Y?" Hem asked. "They come round every Saturday in the summer and chase us out of the pool early, so they can clean it."

Lorraine shook her head.

"No one comes round here but us," Randall said. "We try to scoop out the big stuff." He cupped his hands together and lifted some dead leaves from the corner of the pool.

I couldn't believe Hemingway remembered about going to the Y. Daddy was the one who used to take us, but that was a good two years ago. Before the whiskey took over his breathing and talking. Before Flannery.

I could still remember my eyes and nose watering from all the chlorine they put in the pool. And I could almost feel Daddy's hands, gently wiping over my eyelids. *Blink, Harper. It'll flush it out. Saturdays are free, and they have to put all the chemicals in because of kids like Hem, who use it for a second toilet.* And he'd laughed and scooped Hem up above the water, like Hem couldn't do anything wrong if he'd tried. I had always wanted Daddy to laugh that way with me.

I knelt down and ran my hand along the bumpy edge of the concrete. Daddy used to go in the pool with us. And if we got too close to the deep water, he'd be right behind us. *You're past the line there, Harper Lee.* His voice was slow and easy, and he'd grab me around the middle and tugboat me back to the other side. Just like he'd done with Mama when he came around and rescued her from her old life. He'd scooped her up from that Louisiana bayou. I used to like to imagine him carrying her suitcase for her and carting her away. *Come on with me where I can take care of you, Georgia,* he might have said. *We got nothing but time to hear all those nice stories you have in your head.* If I knew I could have that Daddy back, I'd wait right next to Hem every day.

I stood up and walked to the old blue slide at the end of the pool. The end that was supposed to dip into the pool had snapped off, making it look like you were sliding off a cliff or a big drop-off. I had my foot on the bottom rung of the ladder, and I was thinking on how I might like to try that drop-off, when I saw the sneaky coyote eyes peeking through the opening in the blackberry bushes.

Chapter Eleven

"NO ONE INVITED YOU, Winnie Rae Early." I saw her poke her nosy old self through the opening in the blackberry bushes. "Go right on back through those stickers and find someone who wants your company."

I watched her scrape her arm on one of the blackberry thorns as she moved the rest of the way through the bushes.

"What are you doing with the retarded girl?" Winnie Rae rubbed at her arm and pointed her elbow in Lorraine's direction.

I thought about the special-education room at the end of the long hallway at school where they had the big tricycles and Sebbie Weaver, the girl who still brought her baby doll to school in the fifth grade. "That word is full of meanness, Winnie Rae," I said. I remembered what my teacher had told me back in the third grade. "You don't say 'retarded,' you say 'developmentally delayed,' and Lorraine's not that *at all.*"

I looked at Lorraine, who was willing Winnie Rae back against the sticker bushes with her eyes.

But as usual, nothing stopped Winnie Rae once she got her mouth in motion. "How come you weren't at school today, Harper Lee? Mrs. Rodriguez finished up my poems today. She said they were the best she'd seen."

I'd heard Winnie Rae's story writing before, so I doubted that. She would never take my place. There was no way I was going to let that happen.

"You better get yourself to school tomorrow, Harper Lee." Winnie Rae's coyote eyes zeroed in on my blue notebook on the ground by the pool. "Mrs. Rodriguez is almost to your row."

I felt my heart beating in the pit of my stomach when I thought about Mrs. Rodriguez missing my poems.

"I'll get there when I get there." I tried to remember Mama's exact words as she was telling me she needed me to stay home. It had been just this morning, but it already seemed like so long ago. She had to let me go to school tomorrow.

I stared right through the middle of Winnie Rae's face, which usually made her back off. "What are you doing hanging around here, anyway?"

But I could see Winnie Rae wasn't in a backing-off mood. She took a few steps forward and grabbed hold of the rail on the ladder. "Mama works here. I can be here any time I want."

"Just because your mama owns our house doesn't mean she owns the whole county." My foot was itching to give her a good kick.

"That's not your house anymore, Harper Lee Morgan." I could tell Winnie Rae enjoyed reminding me about that. "Your daddy owes us so much money, Mama says he could've bought and sold the place a few times over."

I thought about Daddy and how our house must've looked to him if he'd happened to turn in his seat as he drove away. I imagined our house getting smaller and smaller in the rear window of his pickup, and all of a sudden it was him I was mad at, and not Winnie Rae Early. Plenty of mad was swirling around my face right about then; maybe even enough to make Winnie Rae go on back the way she'd come in.

But Winnie Rae had a long stubborn streak to her, and her feet stayed planted where they were.

I looked over at the other end of the pool. Everyone was climbing out. Winnie Rae sure knew how to spoil a good time.

Lorraine snatched her towel from the ground and wrapped it around her shoulders. Her eyes said what her words didn't need to.

"I know what you mean, Lorraine." I pressed my lips together and willed my arms to stay at my sides and my feet to stop getting ready to give Winnie Rae Early a good sharp kick. "The other end of this pool has developed a stink to it."

We gathered up our things and made our way back toward the blackberry bushes. Lorraine was good at ignoring people and keeping her temper. She looked right through Winnie Rae, as if she was the missing part of the pool slide.

Winnie Rae gave Lorraine and me her double snake-eye look, where she lets her meanness settle back and simmer for later. And she took off ahead of us, through the bushes, without another word.

I turned to Lorraine. "I hope she caught a good handful of extra-prickly stickers on the way out."

Lorraine smiled.

When we got down the path a ways, Lorraine

stopped to tie up her sneakers and motioned for me to go on.

Randall ran to catch up with me. He glanced back at Lorraine and stared me down hard. "She's not retarded, you know."

"I know that, Randall," I said. "I'd have known that even if you hadn't told me yourself."

He lowered his voice. "She stopped talking right after the fire. It started in her room. In the wires in the wall. She wouldn't move." He made his own legs go stiff and straight. "The firefighter had to carry her out the window."

"They carry you out, too?" Hemingway looked interested, but not scared.

Thinking about Lorraine all frozen and still with the fire in her wall like that made the skin on my arms get prickly.

Randall shook his head. "I wasn't home. I had a sleepover at my cousin's."

Lorraine's arms were straight and tight at her sides when she caught up with us, and I knew she'd heard.

"You want to come over for a while, Hemingway?" Randall rubbed the end of his towel over the top of his head.

Hem started to say yes, but I could tell by his shoulders he was thinking about what time it was.

I answered for him. "Maybe later."

Hemingway's feet automatically started to speed up on the path toward the motel, and I had to take a couple of skips to keep up with him. I looked over my shoulder at Lorraine and Randall. "Thanks for the swim!"

I wondered for a minute where they were going to go. Randall had seemed to find us easily before, but I needed to remember to ask for their room number next time.

For some reason, Hemingway's body knew what time it was. I'd heard in school about the biological time clocks of animals. Hem was like that when it came time to do his waiting for Daddy. His timing was a little off today, though. Probably from being in a new place.

He jogged the rest of the way back to our motel room. He bent his head down and squinted up his eyes when he got to the gravel in front.

"What are you doing?" I unlocked the room and sat down in the doorway.

He moved a piece of gravel with his toe. "I think I see tire tracks. Daddy might have come by looking for us when we were gone."

I clenched my fists up tight, and I could feel my pulse beating in my palms. Maybe Daddy knew what time it was, just like Hem. Maybe he had come back to spill his whiskey all over my new poems. Just in time for this year's contest. I took a couple of slow breaths and I made my shoulders drop down. My imagination tended to run every which way when Daddy crept into my mind.

I went over and took the wet towel from Hem's shoulders. "He doesn't know where we are yet, Hem," I said softly.

He nodded his head hard. "Yes, he does. I gave Winnie Rae a dollar to tell him where we are."

I dug my toes into the gravel when I thought about that mean old Winnie Rae taking Hem's dollar, but I made myself smile. "We weren't gone that long. It's not even quite your usual time. Why don't you change out of those wet clothes and go sit down in the doorway, where it's more comfortable to do your waiting?"

I got him some dry clothes and a graham cracker and he seemed to settle down a bit, so I opened my notebook and sat by the window.

A poem had been forming in my head all day. I didn't have a title for it yet, but I couldn't stop to think one up because my pen was already moving.

Lately I've been wondering what it would be like
To keep all my words inside.
I wonder if they'd come out another way.
Through my pen maybe
Or through a piece of chalk on the sidewalk.
It could actually be safer that way.
The words couldn't hurt anyone.
You could take back all the wrong ones.
You'd just crumple up the paper or
Wait for the rain.

Chapter Twelve

THE RED NUMBERS on the clock read 8:25 when I finally heard Mama's key in the lock. She was so dog-tired she could barely sit herself down at the little table by the window. I had to uncurl her fingers and take the motel key from her hand.

"It's past dinnertime, Mama," I said, "and I'm thinking you probably don't even have any lunch in you."

She smiled and opened her arms for Hem and me. "All I need is my kids."

I wished I could take all the tired out of Mama. I wanted her to sit down with Hem and me and tell us one of her stories. The kind where she changes up all the voices.

Hem wiped the back of his hand across his face

and caught the tail end of his supper. He had a streak of peanut butter that reached from the middle of his cheek to his ear.

Mama pulled a tissue out of the sleeve of her sweater and dabbed at his face with her quick, house-cleaning fingers. They were always soft, thanks to the gloves she wore at work. She hugged Hem. "Did any of it even make it into your belly?"

"You need something in *your* belly, Mama." I nudged my journal to the side and got to work making her up a thick peanut-butter sandwich. I cut it twice so it came out in four little squares. That way she could get it down faster.

She patted my arm and took a big bite.

I put out an apple for dessert. "They had these in a bowl at the front desk."

"They were out for the taking," Hem said, carefully. He wanted to make sure Mama knew we came by it honestly. He'd had a problem, a couple of years back, of coming home with extra things from the supermarket. Bunches of grapes and kitchen sponges and such. For some reason he'd loved those bright yellow kitchen sponges, and they always managed to make their way under his shirt. Mama finally caught wind of it when he had about fifteen or twenty of them laid out side by side as a squishy road for his little cars.

Mama had been fit to be tied when she'd seen his stolen yellow road. But Daddy just smiled and shook his head. *Ease up a little, Georgia,* he'd said to Mama. *He's not a criminal, for heaven's sake. He's just a little kid.* And Daddy had taken Hem's hands in his and leaned in close to him. *From now on, you keep your hands tight in your pockets when you go into the store with your mother, Hem.*

I had known without a doubt, if it had been me doing the taking, Daddy would've marched me right down to the police station.

I wondered if Mama was doing some remembering of her own.

She smiled a sad sort of smile, the kind where you start one up and don't quite finish it, and leaned back in her chair. "I don't know what I'd do without you two." She pulled off a piece of bread crust and chewed it slowly, as if it was the fancy, expensive kind from the bakery downtown. That was the thing about Mama. She acted like I'd spent all day on dinner.

But then she reached for her white notepad, and she started back up with her worrying. As soon as she got her pencil out and began adding and subtracting, her chewing got short and fast and her shoulders hunched up around her ears.

When I saw her eyebrow make a crooked line across her forehead, I knew I wasn't going to school tomorrow, either. I had thought only Daddy could ruin the contest for me this year, but I guessed I was wrong.

I blew short, quick breaths out of my mouth, up toward my eyes, the kind that help the tears stay back, and I went into the bathroom and pulled the door shut behind me. I sat down on the toilet and closed my eyes and tried to pretend I was back in my old bedroom. Before it ended up on our front lawn.

MAMA DIDN'T EVEN bother waking me up to tell me. The first thing I saw in the morning was the chocolates on the little table by the window. Mama sometimes got them from one of her housecleaning jobs. Miss Oakley left them for her when she worked extra. The square gold box was scooted toward the edge of the table, and a piece of paper from Mama's notepad was tucked underneath at one corner. She had drawn a heart in the middle of the paper with my name in it.

Usually, I was quick to hide those chocolates before Hem got his hands on them. But today I didn't even care. I just wanted to get to school.

When Hem woke up, he didn't reach for his handwriting book first thing, like he usually did. He pulled his pants on and went right over to the front window. "They come by yet?" He grabbed the shirt Mama had laid out from the back of the chair and pulled it over his head.

"It's too early, Hem." This was the time when I usually got out my clothes for school and put my lunch together. I looked at my backpack propped against the wall. My blue notebook was leaning against it, and I thought about Mrs. Rodriguez calling my row to come up to her desk.

Then I saw her skipping over my empty desk and moving to the next row.

I grabbed my comb. "Come on, Hem." I handed it to him. "Go into the bathroom and run this through your hair. And don't forget to brush your teeth."

I made up a quick peanut-butter sandwich and wrapped it in one of the washcloths from the bathroom. Then I grabbed two apples and put everything in the front pocket of my backpack and tied my shoes. "Get your backpack. We're going out for a bit." I opened Hem's plastic pencil box and checked for markers and extra pencils and dropped it into his backpack with his handwriting book and drawing pad.

Hem put his backpack over both shoulders and fastened the lower strap around his belly. "Can we see if Randall wants to go, too?"

"Not this time." I checked the clock. "Let's get a move on."

He marched along beside me up to the main road with his hands holding tightly to the straps of his backpack.

I reached for his hand. "Hold on to me now, Hem. The traffic's pretty busy up on the main road."

The traffic was more than busy. The cars were going by like on the highway, and I almost turned us both back to the motel. But then I saw the yellow bus slowing down as it came around the corner, and I forgot about being scared. I took a step forward and put my hand up for the driver to stop.

As soon as the doors folded open, Hem started up the steps.

"He's a little young for high school, don't you think?" The bus driver took a sip of her coffee and smiled at us.

I climbed to the second step and took hold of a strap on Hem's backpack. A boy looked to be asleep in the first seat. He rested his head on his coat up against the window, and I could see he was growing himself a mustache.

The bus driver took another sip of her coffee and wiped her mouth on the back of her hand. "Elementary bus'll be by in a little while. But you two might want to wait up at the bus shelter. This isn't a very safe place to stand." She pointed down the road to a red-and-white wooden shack with a long bench.

"Thanks." I tugged at Hem's backpack and stepped back onto the gravel next to the road. A girl threw a candy wrapper out through the window at me as the bus took off.

Hem bounced on the balls of his feet. "You didn't tell me we were going to ride the bus today!"

"Yeah, well, I just thought of it." I pulled him toward the red-and-white shack.

I handed him an apple from my backpack and sat down on the bench. Then I rested my backpack on my lap and put my hand inside to check for my poems. I knew my blue notebook without even looking. The edge corners were soft, like Mama's cotton housecoat, from turning the pages back and forth so often. As soon as Mrs. Rodriguez checked my poems, I could turn in my permission slip and I'd be home free. I wouldn't have to worry about getting back to school until the day of the contest, when I'd be reading my poems at the microphone up on the auditorium stage.

I heard the bus coming and I pulled Hemingway to his feet.

Chapter Thirteen

WHEN THE DOORS folded open, Hem didn't move forward even one step. And I didn't blame him. The bus driver looked like the cranky cashier from the last lane at the supermarket when Mama was counting out her coupons.

He leaned sideways in his seat and put his hand on the lever that closed the door. "This isn't one of my stops." He reached his hand out. "You got your paperwork?"

"I got papers." Hem took off his backpack and rifled around inside. He pulled out his best drawing of the side of our house with the dirt pile for his trucks. I knew him to be plenty proud of that drawing, and I wanted to give that bus driver a good hard kick in his big old bus seat when he didn't even take a short look at it.

I put my hand on Hem's shoulder. "We need a special paper?" My permission-slip paper seemed to be burning a hole right through my backpack and onto my side.

The bus driver took a loud breath and rolled his eyes to the ceiling of the bus. "Any unscheduled stop has to come with paperwork from the office." He checked his watch and shooed us away from the bus with the back of his hand.

Then, before I could even think on what he had said, he snapped those bus doors shut and pulled back onto the road.

"How was I supposed to know?" I didn't mean to sound angry at Hem, but my voice came out that way without my even trying. "I've always been a walker. I've never had to set foot on the school bus."

I had seen Sarah Lynn Newhart staring at me, her nose pressed up against the window as the bus roared away. She could've said something. She always had her hand up to give an answer at school. Friends were supposed to help each other out, even if they were just school friends. I wanted to throw something at her window, and I stooped down and ran my hand over a smooth gray pebble. But then I just got plain sad. She was probably glad I didn't get let on the bus. She sat down the row from me, and she knew Mrs. Rodriguez would get to her poems quicker if she skipped over me.

My stomach growled loudly, and I sat myself back down on the worn red bench and took a bite of my apple.

Hem hung back a bit. The angry part of my voice always scared him.

I patted the seat beside me. "I'm not mad at you, Hem. I'm sorry. I need some time to cool the angry feelings off my brain and think about things."

Hem was never one to hold a grudge. He plopped himself down next to me and started chewing at his own apple. He turned sideways toward me and hugged his knees up on the bench. "If you're needing some cooling off, we could maybe go swimming again."

Hem's idea wasn't half bad. I had been wanting to check out that cut-off slide without Winnie Rae Early stinking up the pool area. A few trips down that slide could possibly sort through the jumble in my brain and set me to thinking straight. I had to come up with a way to get back to school.

I stood up and swung my backpack over one shoulder. "Okay, then, Hem. Let's go get our towels."

As we made our way back down to our motel room, I tried to ignore thoughts of any poems, old or newly forming in my head. But that's the thing about poems and stories. Once they start taking shape inside your brain, there's no stopping or ignoring them. They tend to nag at you until your hand gets around to finding a pen and writing them down.

"Mama said always lock the door, even when we're there." Hem pushed the door open and stepped inside.

I'd been so worried about getting on the school bus I hadn't locked the motel room. Which meant that anyone could've gotten inside while we were gone. And I was plenty annoyed with what I found on the floor in front of our TV.

"Hey, Randall." Hemingway tossed his backpack on the bed and took another bite of his apple.

Randall had cartoons on, and he was chewing away on one of our graham crackers. "Lorraine said it wasn't polite to come in without an invite, but I told her you wouldn't mind." He shook some broken pieces of graham cracker into his mouth and crumpled up the waxed-paper wrapper. "I knew you'd be right back or you wouldn't have left the door unlocked."

He was pretty smart for a kid that had had so much school vacation.

"You mean Lorraine's found her words?" I couldn't believe I had missed it.

Randall shook his head. "Lorraine talks at you with her pen and her hands and sometimes her eyes. You'll find out once you get to know her better. You catch her with her pad of paper or her arms moving about, and there's no breaking loose from her."

Sure enough, when I looked outside, she was standing off in the corner of the parking lot with Dorothy. Her hand was moving back and forth across her notepad. She must've been used to all that quick writing, because she didn't even stop to shake her hand out.

"Want to go swimming?" Hem already had his towel around his neck.

It was a good thing Randall had broken in. I wasn't so sure I could find the opening in the black-berry bushes again. I would've walked right past it that first time, if Randall and Lorraine hadn't shown us where to turn.

"In a minute." Randall reached down to the floor and picked up a thin, square paperback book. On the cover were two kids with bikes. *We Ride and Play*, it said across the top. "Could you show me how to read this?"

I took the book from him and opened up the front cover. PROPERTY OF MOUNTAINRIDGE SCHOOL DISTRICT was stamped in dark blue ink across the bottom of the first page.

He must've known what that stamp said, because his eyes got real wide and started jumping all around. "I'm not keeping it forever. I'm going to give it back once I learn how to read it." He tapped the middle of the page. "We were just getting started on this one in reading group when our vacation started. Mr. Verone said we could take our book home over the weekend and practice with our parents. I didn't know my vacation was starting after the weekend or I would have left it there."

Hemingway was pulling at his towel like he was anxious to get to the pool, but I could tell he was liking the looks of that book. He had been getting excited about learning some words of his own, and he moved in closer to check out the front cover.

I sat them down on the floor on either side of me and opened the book on my lap. I pointed to the first word. "You know that one, Hemingway."

"'I'!" Randall shouted it out before Hemingway could get his mouth around it.

"That's right," I said. "But hush up and give Hem a chance with the next one."

He didn't look to be hushing up, so I gave him a Mrs. Rodriguez look and he pressed his lips together hard.

I pointed to the next word. "This one's a hard one, so I'm going to give it to you for now. It's 'ride.'" I tapped the page. "Remember that one, because it comes up a lot in this book."

The book didn't have a whole lot of plot to it. It was all about people riding their bikes like the picture on the cover. But Randall and Hemingway couldn't wait to turn each page. New words were always like that for me, too.

Mrs. Rodriguez thought fifth-graders had lots of wasted space in their brains. She made us write down a new word each day. We had long lists rolled up in our desks. Every time we got to the bottom of a page, she'd let us tape another sheet across the bottom.

I looked at the Knotty Pine alarm clock. The class was probably doing spelling right then. I imagined myself sitting at my desk, adding to my list and finding the perfect word to use in my new poem. I could almost feel that rolled-up paper in my hand.

I let out a long breath and wondered if I'd ever get to add to my list again.

Chapter Fourteen

AFTER A WHILE, I said, "That's enough for now." I closed Randall's book and handed it to him.

He pushed my hand back. "Why don't I leave it with you? Then you can teach me some more tomorrow and I won't have to worry about losing track of it." He held up my backpack. "You could keep it in here, maybe."

He was kind of nervy, that Randall, but I think he was what Mama called "hungry for words." Mama said our people were like that. We could never get enough stories.

He looked at me with his eyebrows up, like he was getting ready to beg. "Sometimes things get wet at my house."

I couldn't figure out why things would get wet in their motel room, but I took the book back and looked at the side wall, stacked high with all we'd been able to carry in our car. "All right. I guess I could keep it with Hem's handwriting books and such."

He smiled like I'd just given him a handful of cash. "Thanks."

I stuffed my towel in my backpack and tucked my motel key into the little zippered pouch in the front. When we got outside, Dorothy and her wheelchair were gone, but Lorraine was still there. She sat on a block of concrete that marked the end of a parking space. She had her sketchpad on her lap, and she was drawing with markers.

"Mama buys her all the paper and markers she wants," Randall said. "She thinks drawing might help her get her words out." He pointed at a marker on the ground in front of Lorraine. "She never uses the orange. She doesn't throw it away or anything. She just takes it out first thing and leaves it there until she's done."

I knew why she did it. The orange probably made her think of the fire. When she took out the orange, she was most likely reminding herself not to think about it.

Lorraine saw us coming and started stuffing her markers back in the box.

"Hey, Lorraine." I made a point of not looking at the orange marker.

She smiled at me and wiggled her fingers hello.

"They want to go swimming again." Randall smoothed his hand over his name tag. "We'll have to change into yesterday's stuff." He pulled his shirt down. "Mama hates it when we make too much laundry."

Lorraine nodded and stood up to lead the way. But she didn't stop at any of the motel rooms to change her clothes, which I thought was real strange. She didn't seem like the kind of person who would ignore what her mama said.

Then, when she led us over the crumbled concrete around back and down the narrow path past all the blackberry bushes, I got really confused. And Randall kept chatting away to Hem, as if he didn't even notice how far we'd gone.

"Hey, Lorraine." I cleared my throat loudly, in case her thoughts were getting jumbled inside her head, along with her words. "Haven't we gone too far?"

She smiled and shook her head. She didn't look confused at all.

"It's just a little farther up." Randall pointed

down the path, where the trees were getting farther apart.

I was starting to ask him what he was talking about when I realized they didn't live in the motel at all. I saw where they lived.

It was beautiful and Lorraine knew it. I could tell by the proud way the corners of her mouth tilted up when she saw I'd noticed it.

At least half a dozen tents were scattered through the trees. Some even had a little indoor furniture they were using for the outside. Up ahead, a man sat next to a red square of a tent. He leaned back in a brown plaid armchair, reading his newspaper.

I didn't know how I knew, but I was sure as anything that the green tent with the squared-off top was theirs. As soon as I laid eyes on it, I got that same happy, relaxed feeling I'd gotten when I first met Lorraine.

Someone had added on to the tent to make it bigger. Clotheslines were strung from one tree to another right next to the tent. Hanging from each of the clotheslines was the most beautiful cloth I'd ever seen. Greens, yellows, and reds on one piece, and turquoise, purple, and royal blue on another, bursting out from the center of each cloth as if the colors were traveling out to meet us.

"It's batik." Randall said it slowly, like it was two words—"buh teek." His voice had the same pride in it as Lorraine's eyes and smile. "Mama makes the cloth. She learned from her mother."

"It's like a fancy painting." I wanted to touch it, but I didn't want Lorraine to get mad. Some people didn't like anyone touching their stuff. The only thing I didn't much care for was the long black plastic tarp that hung overhead of it all. But I figured it to be their rain protection.

Lorraine pointed at what looked like bicycle tracks in the dirt.

"Mama's at the food bank," Randall said. "They got extra cheese this week. She always gets them to give her the extras, and she passes it out to the people that can't make it down there."

I looked across the way at a woman eating at a card table. She sat in a knobby dining-room chair that looked just like the ones we had from my grandmother.

"We're not usually allowed to have people over when she's gone." Randall looked behind the first batik cloth as if he was checking to be sure. "But

Mama won't mind you being here. You're special company. She knows all about your story writing."

Lorraine nodded and held back the other cloth so I could walk past.

When I went behind the cloth, I gulped down a big burst of air. Bright color was everywhere. But there was no orange. Their mama must definitely have known how Lorraine felt about orange.

Purple, green, and pink paper lanterns were hanging up high from one end of the tent to the next. They looked like the kind we made in school last year for Chinese New Year.

But the floor was the absolute best. More of the batik cloth was covering the ground, and all around the edges of the room were dozens of pillows in all my favorite colors from the crayon box. The ones with fancy names, like "periwinkle" and "azure." I knew those to be the exact colors, because the pillows had name tags, just like Lorraine and Randall. In fact, everything there had a name tag, from the tree stumps to the big sitting rock in the corner. Some of them were fresh and crisp, like on the front of the tree-stump cushion, and some of them had the corners coming up, as if they'd been there awhile.

I couldn't help myself. I had to sit down on that

tree-stump cushion and get a close-up view of the batik cloth behind it. It was as if my favorite poems traveled out of my brain and onto that cloth.

Lorraine smiled and looked at Randall.

"She knows how to make it, too," Randall said. "But I'm not allowed. You have to use hot wax."

Lorraine shooed Randall and Hem away with a quick flick of the back of her hand.

"You go wait out front," Randall told Hem. "I'm going to change into my swimming clothes."

Lorraine unzipped the cloth door, and she and Randall went off into the main part of the tent. I stood so I was in the very middle of the batik room. I leaned my head back and let all the color zigzag into my brain.

It was something blue and flower-shaped that snapped my brain to attention. It was pushed to the edge of the tent and almost completely covered in cloth.

I knew what it was before I'd even lifted up the cloth, because there was no mistaking the bright green paint and blue flower decals.

Chapter Fifteen

HEM WALKED BACK into the tent, and I wondered how long it would take him to recognize it.

I ran my finger along the outside edges of a daisy decal, and Randall came up beside me and smiled.

"Mama brought that home for Lorraine last night." He peeled back a corner of the cloth and patted the front of the top drawer. "She said it might be hard to fit it in the car when we leave here, but she couldn't pass it up. So it's an early birthday present."

Lorraine nodded, her eyes smiling real big.

"Mama said you got to jump at a bargain when you see one, and that yard sale had a whole slew of them." Randall smoothed his hand along the side of the dresser.

Lorraine looked plenty proud of that dresser, and

I could see she wanted me to be all excited for her, like a good friend would. She pointed at a daisy decal.

But she didn't need to point it out to me. I knew every petal with my eyes closed, since I was the one that had put all of them on there. Those daisy decals were one of my birthday presents two years ago. I'd put them on with tape first, before I'd actually peeled off the backs. I'd wanted to get them spaced right. Once you stick them on, they're there forever. At least I thought so. Unless the entire dresser gets moved.

I couldn't breathe quite right.

It wasn't till Hem finally got himself a good look that the tears started in the corners of my eyes.

"That looks just like your dresser, Harper Lee." Hem tried to get closer, but Lorraine blocked his way. I didn't blame her, though. That dresser was now her birthday present, and she didn't want any grubby little-boy fingerprints dirtying it up.

I put my head down and pressed my fingertips up against the middle of my forehead and tried to keep the tears back. "Come on, Hem. We've got to go."

"What do you mean?" His voice told me he was getting ready to put up a fight. "We're going swimming. Remember?"

I'd never been a very good liar, so I tried not to look at Lorraine, or my dresser. "I can't believe I forgot about our appointment." I lifted up my wrist like there was a watch on it.

"Appointment?" That got Hem's attention right away. "Mama didn't say nothing about a doctor today."

"You guys come by later." I waved at Lorraine and Randall. "Couple hours or so." I hooked my arm through Hem's elbow and pulled him out of the tent before the wailing started. All Hem had to do was think on the word "doctor," and he started screaming his head off.

I pulled him out of earshot of the tent and gave his arm a good squeeze.

"Mama didn't say nothing about a doctor today," he said again, his voice all high and squeaky.

I bent down so I was about two inches from his forehead and took his face in my hands. "Settle down, now, Hem. All I said was 'appointment.' We are not going to the doctor, so relax. I can't think when you go on with your voice all squeaky like that."

Everything was coming at me in a jumble right then, and it was hard for my brain to figure out what to think about first. When we drove away from our house, I hadn't thought anything would happen to all we had left behind. I had tucked it all into a safe place in my mind. In fact, when I'd thought about it, I'd made myself picture everything the way it always was, in its rightful place in our house. Not being sifted through in Winnie Rae Early's camping trailer, or stacked in a pile in her old shed. Or worse.

Hem looked at me, his mouth wide open like he was still getting ready for a good scream.

I leaned in close. "No shots today. All right?"

He nodded slowly and spit his breath out, one burst at a time, as if he wasn't quite ready to believe me yet.

"All right, then." I pulled some gum out of the pocket of my sweatshirt and handed him a stick. "Here. Get your jaws moving on this. We've got some walking to do, and you've got to get your energy up."

I unwrapped a stick for myself and tried to concentrate on getting a good chew going. I couldn't let Hem see me cry. He was riled up enough as it was. I tried to think about how I was getting back to school, but I couldn't push the dresser out of my mind. I could still feel the stickiness of the daisy decals as I peeled off the back and found the perfect spot for each one. I remembered how those decals fancied it right up so it didn't look like a baby dresser anymore. I had been so proud of the way it looked. Even Daddy had said how nice it was.

It was at least a half-hour's walk to our old place, and another day I might have actually enjoyed it. I was feeling warm enough to unzip my sweatshirt, and there were almost no cars on the road. But there was a nagging, heavy feeling moving from side to side in my stomach, and Hem cranked up a good whine by the time we were twenty minutes into it. Every time Hem's high voice started to get to me, I kicked a rock off into the ditch beside the road.

I didn't know why, but the walk down the last road to our house felt different. I'd gone over that same path at least two times a day for the last few years, but today it seemed unfamiliar somehow. I had passed the same three maple trees, with the branches that tangled into one another, but it almost seemed as if they were telling me I didn't have a right to be there anymore.

When we got to the end of our driveway, that heavy feeling dropped right down to my sneakers. I looked at Hem, and I could tell that he felt it, too. He stood with his mouth open a tiny bit.

The van in the driveway was one I'd seen before,

but I couldn't straightaway remember where. It was green, with a dented-in spot over the taillight. Someone had put a bumper sticker on the back to try to hide the dent. *My child is an honor student at Kennedy Elementary.*

The feeling in my body got shakier, because that bumper sticker went and reminded me about my poems and how I wasn't at school to show them to Mrs. Rodriguez.

I stood at the end of our driveway, my toes touching the curb. And I heard a small sound coming from behind me. It was a soft, whimpering sound, and when I turned around, I could see it was coming from Hem.

He was staring at his dirt pile by the corner of the house, and I saw a little boy sitting to the side. He was running trucks through the dirt pile.

But it wasn't the little boy that was making that sound come out of Hem's mouth. It was seeing those trucks. Hem's trucks. The ones that we had packed away in Winnie Rae Early's camping trailer.

We had been in a bit of a hurry that day, but I could still picture them in the waxy brown banana box. Resting on top of my dresser with the daisy decals.

Before I could even think about stopping him, Hem was standing knee-deep in that dirt pile. He held one truck in each hand, and the little boy was screaming his head off.

Then Hem was screaming his head off, too. "Get your snotty nose out of my dirt pile! You're ruining my best roads!"

And a woman was making her way down the front steps and across to the side yard. "What in the world is going on out here?"

I should've grabbed Hem and his trucks and run on back to the motel, but I was frozen. My feet had stopped still when I laid eyes on that orange sign.

Chapter Sixteen

I'D RECOGNIZE Mrs. Early's writing anywhere, after all those notices she'd tacked up on our front windows and door. Her "L"s always lay down a bit, like they were reclining in a lawn chair. The sign itself was tilted to the side against the garbage can, so you had to put your ear down to your shoulder to properly read the YARD SALE part.

"Give that back to him, now." The lady waggled her pointer finger at Hem, but Hem held on to his truck as tightly as if it was a life preserver.

She looked to be getting ready to grab it out of his hand, but Hem took a quick step sideways and she almost fell in the dirt pile.

She said a word I'm not inclined to repeat, and I remembered how I knew that van in the driveway. It belonged to Mrs. Early's sister. Winnie Rae's aunt.

She wasn't nearly as fat as Winnie Rae's mother, but she was twice as mean about the mouth. Those swear words of hers had a bite to them.

I did what I did when Mrs. Early let loose with her curses. I turned sideways and let them blow right past. But what I couldn't shake was the strangeness I felt seeing someone else living in our house and digging in our dirt pile.

When I looked at Winnie Rae's nasty aunt and her grubby cousin, it all started to make sense, and I got a numb feeling all the way down to my fingertips. "Mrs. Early probably had them moving their stuff in the back door as we were moving our stuff off the front lawn." I said it to Hem, but I was looking right at Winnie Rae's aunt. They had probably been planning it ever since they put the first sign up on our door.

Hem looked as if he didn't understand it all. Another kid running Hem's own trucks through his dirt pile just plain confused him. But not as much as the van in the driveway. I followed Hem's eyes to the green van.

His voice came out soft and small. "That might be Daddy's new car."

The toy truck in his hand tumbled slowly to the ground, and he started to head in the direction of the front porch, but I grabbed his arm.

He tried to shake me off. "Daddy's inside." He said it all quiet, as if he was afraid he might wake Daddy from a nap.

"Hem . . . Hemingway . . ." I tried to block his way, but he was plenty quick.

I saw his eyes getting wide and glassy and a little like a crazed animal as he ran to the front steps. "Daddy's inside . . . Daddy's inside. . . ." He kept repeating it over and over again, getting louder each time.

Seeing as Winnie Rae's aunt wasn't half as enormous as her sister, she got to the front door before Hem, and she grabbed him by the shoulders. "I have no idea what you're ranting about, boy, but you need to take all that crazy talk back down my stairs and leave me and my son alone!"

I would've been perfectly fine with her just blocking his way, but seeing her grab him by the shoulders sent loose the crazy part of me.

"Mama! That boy had his dirty hands on my truck! He bent back my finger!" Winnie Rae's cousin was trying to make it up those steps carrying a couple of Hem's biggest trucks and show his mama his pointer finger at the same time. So he wasn't too hard to push to the side when I went to rescue Hem.

I made straight for Winnie Rae's aunt. "Nobody's going to grab on to Hem like that except me!" I told it to her good and hard, because it definitely looked as if she was capable of digging in with her fingernails. There was nothing worse than a fingernail grabber.

Which was why I had to step on her toe with the heel of my sneaker.

She gave out a sound that came straight from her belly and sounded as if someone had pumped a chunk of air out of her.

I had a backup plan that involved her knee, but luckily she let go of Hem after one stomp.

He had started whimpering, and he didn't put up a fight when I led him down the stairs and out to the curb.

Mrs. Early's sister was speeding up her swears, but her boy was screaming louder than everybody.

"Get him, Mama! Get them both!" He was holding

a skinned elbow, so I figured she probably wouldn't bother coming after me.

Sure enough, she scooped him up and hauled him on into the house, with barely a look back.

I sat on the curb and pulled Hemingway down on my lap and rubbed his back like Mama sometimes did for me. I closed my eyes and made my breath trickle out slowly. When Hem's whimpering got quieter, I scooted him next to me. "You understand that's not our house anymore, right?" I said it quietly, but with a strong voice, so he'd listen and believe me.

He looked me in the eye and took a few quick, shaky gulps of air, but he didn't say anything.

"Daddy couldn't be inside, because he doesn't know those people, right?" I nodded toward our old house.

"He had my trucks." Hem took another shaky gulp of air. "That kid had my trucks."

I patted his back. "I know, Hem. I know." I got up and went over to the garbage can.

I kicked the YARD SALE sign to the ground and looked around on the grass.

The yard sale itself was over, because all that was

left were the broken pieces. The parts that had been stepped on or ignored. Everything was tossed in a long pile, waiting for the trash collector to come by and haul it away. I had never had a fire like Lorraine, but this seemed worse somehow. The fire had been an accident, but everything here had been on purpose, and it made me feel sick inside to see the bits and pieces of our life all torn up and scattered.

Hem walked toward the back of the pile and pulled out our old ceramic towel rack from the bathroom. He ran his hand along the purple forget-me-nots I'd painted on one end. "How come they're throwing away our stuff?"

I thought about my green dresser with the daisy decals and I shook my head. "I think they were selling it." I remembered Winnie Rae Early coming across the lawn with her Radio Flyer wagon and I wondered if she'd already had the price tags made out.

All of a sudden, I was dog-tired, and the only thing I wanted to do was see Mama and sit down with my pen.

Hem didn't say much on the way home, which was good, because there was a poem writing itself out in my mind the whole way back.

Dear Flannery

It's a good thing you aren't around
To see this, Flannery.
I'm glad you can't see someone else
Sitting around on our front porch
And digging through our dirt pile.
That would have been
Your very own dirt pile in a couple of years.
I would've helped you make roads with your fingers
And haul water for the lakes
In the middle.
And when you got old enough,
That green dresser with the daisy decals
Would have been yours, too.

Chapter Seventeen

WE WERE ONLY about five minutes away from the motel when Hem started up with his whining again. I just wanted to get back and work on my school plan, so I held tightly around his wrist and pulled him along behind me, trying to block out the sound.

But when we got to the next bend in the road, he stopped dead still and seemed to bury his heels right into the asphalt.

"Come on, Hem." I pulled a little harder, but all it did was put him off-balance.

He rocked forward and back on the balls of his feet a few times and dug his heels in hard. "I'm tired and my legs are done walking."

There was only one thing that would get him moving again. "It's almost time to do your waiting,"

I said. "It's just about time to do your waiting for Daddy."

He shook his head, because he knew I was wrong. "I got three or four hours still." His inside clock never failed. "Besides," he said, "it's even better to be out here. I can see all the cars that go by." He kicked over a wide curve of old tire that had blown off a truck and sat down on it.

It was big enough for the both of us, so I breathed out a long puff of air and sat down next to him. I had to admit, I was tired of walking, too. And my stomach was letting me know it was past lunchtime. I pulled the peanut-butter sandwich out of my backpack and unfolded the washcloth.

"Here." I handed the squished part to Hem, because I knew he wouldn't notice. Sure enough, he pointed it in the direction of his mouth and took a bite.

I was starting to wish for something to wash it down with when I saw her. The last person in the world I wanted to see standing in front of me.

"Not in school again, I noticed." Winnie Rae Early walked herself on over, without one hint of an invitation. "The school nurse has been calling your house," she said. "But I told Mrs. Rodriguez you're not sick. You just don't live there no more."

The thing was, I felt like I was sick right then. I was imagining Mrs. Rodriguez giving my desk away. Or emptying it out and putting it in the hallway, for the custodian to drag off.

Winnie Rae kept right on talking, not stopping for any rest breaks. That's what guilty people did, I'd noticed. They kept the words coming, so you didn't get a chance to accuse them.

"I got permission to ride the morning kindergarten bus to the motel." She was talking as if I cared one ounce about what she did with her day. "Mama told the school I had an important doctor's appointment and she didn't have a car to pick me up." She talked out of the side of her mouth, like she was sharing some big secret with Hem and me. "But really she's getting off work early and taking me to her hairdresser to get my hair permed. We are trying out a new hairstyle. If we don't like it, we still have plenty of time to switch to something different. She wants me to look nice at the hospital when the new baby comes."

I raised one eyebrow at her, because who cared

about what she looked like, anyway? Her enormous mother was having the baby.

She fluffed the frizzy tuft of hair at the side of her head. "Miss Cynthia didn't have any more evening appointments, so Mama took me out of school." She looked me dead in the eye with those beady pig eyes of hers. "I didn't leave till *after* Mrs. Rodriguez had me practice reading my poems in front of the class." The left corner of her mouth always got to twitching to the side when she was lying. "She said I read better than anyone she'd heard in all her years of teaching school."

I knew Mrs. Rodriguez hadn't said any of that, I knew it in my heart. But my mind was asking, what if she had? Maybe Daddy was right. Maybe my words really didn't matter to anyone.

I'd had enough. Winnie Rae was getting to me so bad, my fingers were tightening themselves into hard fists. Those daisy decals were swimming around in my head, and I hated Winnie Rae Early more than a person ought to hate someone. I stood up so the toes of my sneakers were getting ready to bump up against hers.

"You stole my dresser." I said the words slowly, and evenly, so she wouldn't miss one bit of what I was saying. "You took it and sold it and it wasn't yours to be selling."

She took a step back and looked to be gathering herself up to leave. But then she leaned in again so I could smell her lying Early breath. "My mama says we had plenty of right to it." Her evil eyes were pinholes. "She said we could consider it as a tiny drop in the big bucket of rent your daddy owes."

She had torn open the Daddy wound, but somehow all I felt was a strong, sad anger at Daddy for giving Winnie Rae a good reason. He had made it all right for the Earlys to do what they did. And he'd gotten off free of charge. He'd taken everything he cared about with him, so it was all safe from the Earlys' thieving hands.

And then, even though Winnie Rae knew she had me with that one, she had to keep on with her venomous viper words. "Besides," she said, "I needed to get *my* daddy a birthday present. I needed some quick cash. He works long hours driving across the entire United States of America in his eighteen-wheeler." She shrugged. "You got plenty of dresser drawers at the motel, anyway. What would you be needing that ratty old green dresser for?"

My toes were itching to kick at her legs. They

were so close in front of me, it wouldn't be much of a reach. But I knew it might really have been Daddy I was kicking.

She finally stopped for a breath of air, and I didn't think she meant to, but she looked at me. Her eyes found mine, and her words held still in the air between us. She stared for a minute and looked as if someone had pressed her *Stop* button. After a good while, she took a sharp breath and spoke. "I wasn't going to let her sell it."

"What?" She wasn't making any sense.

"The dresser." Winnie Rae's shoulders hunched forward, and her voice had gotten so quiet I had to move in till we were practically sharing the same puff of air.

She bent down and unzipped the front pocket of her book bag. She held up two daisy decals, one in each hand. "I tried to save them all for you, but Mama would've noticed. The dresser wouldn't have looked right with them all peeled off."

She held her hands out until I took the decals from her. "I knew how much you liked it."

I almost never had trouble thinking up words for Winnie Rae Early, but my mind was having a hard time with this one. A nasty Winnie Rae was a lot easier to deal with. And her eyebrows were raised up as if she was surprised by her own words.

But then Hem took my mind and my feet in another direction. He was up and waving his arms over his head at a white pickup. And he was a good three feet into the street.

"Hem!" I grabbed him tight around the middle and pulled him back to the side of the road. I could feel my pulse thudding on the roof of my mouth and a tingly buzzing inside my ears.

"He's slowing down!" Hem tried to wrestle himself free, but this time it was me digging my feet into the asphalt.

I had to admit, Hem had a pretty good eye. That truck was the spitting image of Daddy's. Except there was a lady driving it. And she was not the least bit smiling as she slowed down and unrolled her window.

She jabbed her finger in the air in our direction. "What's wrong with you kids? It's a good thing I was paying attention, or I could've mowed you right down!"

I didn't have a whole lot to say to that, and, luckily, neither did Hemingway. His body had gone kind of limp, and he was studying the dirt by his feet as if it was the most interesting thing in the world.

I hugged him close to me and kissed the side of his face. Breathing in his sweaty, Hemingway smell made my heart start to slow back down to normal.

The woman shook her head and mentioned something about school as she was rolling her window back up.

As I watched the woman drive off, I noticed Winnie Rae had taken the opportunity to hightail it out of there. She was a good twenty yards down the road toward the motel.

I shook my head and got a tighter grip on Hem's hand. I bent down so my eyes were staring in the dead centers of his. "Listen here, Hemingway."

He must have heard something sharper in my voice, because he didn't look away. Not for even one second.

"Mama put me in charge of you, and you're going to have to stick close by. You hear?"

He nodded slowly.

"I know you got more sense than to be running out in front of cars," I said. "Mama taught you that back when you were about two years old."

"But Daddy . . ." He pointed toward the street.

"That wasn't Daddy." I squeezed his wrist so he'd

be sure to listen. "I don't want to talk about Daddy for a while, you hear?"

He looked confused, but he nodded.

"I don't want to be thinking or talking about Daddy for the rest of today. Maybe longer." I said it loudly, so I'd remember it, myself.

"Come on," I said. "Let's go back and see if we can find Randall. Maybe we can do some more reading in that book of his."

He didn't answer, but I felt him give my hand a little bit of a squeeze.

I thought about Mama out front of our old house, bone-tired, trying to sort through everything we owned. There was no way I was going to tell her about my dresser or any part of the Earlys' yard sale. I just couldn't. Mama had way too much to worry about already. I wanted to take some of that worry away and give it to Mrs. Early or Winnie Rae. Let them know what it was like, for once.

I pulled Hem farther off the road. It was harder to walk on all the loose dirt and sharp little rocks, but I wasn't taking any chances on him darting out into traffic again.

"Someone's cooking breakfast." Hem pointed the

tip of his nose up at the sky and took a snorty breath. "Sausages, maybe."

I glanced off to our left, but there wasn't much to see except thick clusters of trees with the new leaves partway grown in. It was a little late for breakfast, and I couldn't picture anyone cooking up some pancakes in the middle of the sticker bushes. The road dipped down into a ditch to the left of us, and this seemed to be a good place for snakes and such.

Hem must've been thinking the same thing, because his foot took a little sidestep and his hand was looking to sneak away from me. "Don't you even think about it." I tightened my grip on his fingers.

There was a road up ahead, and as we got closer, I could see it wasn't a main one. It was just clumpy dirt. Not good for cars, but fine for people walking.

"Did you notice that road up there, Hem?" I pointed toward the start of the dirt road. "If I'm guessing right, it will take us out on the other side of the tent houses." I picked up a rock and bent down, drawing a long line in the dirt. "See? This is the big, busy road. And this is the motel over here." I drew a rectangle in the dirt.

Hem bent down beside me.

"We usually go around back of the motel and

down the sticker-bush path past the pool, and we come up on Randall and Lorraine's from the right." I drew a line branching off the big road. "I'm thinking, if we take this dirt road up ahead here, we're bound to come up on the tent houses from the left."

Hem nodded and smiled. "A shortcut."

"You're going to have to take a run and a jump for it off this main road, though." I pointed at the ditch. "I don't want you slogging through that snake pit." I hadn't seen one single snake, but I had to keep Hem's legs moving.

The old road had chunks of broken-up asphalt with weeds starting to make their way up in the spaces and cracks in between. Early-spring crabgrass and moss felt soft and bumpy under our feet. Before time and weather got to it, I could see it had been a regular road.

"Keep a lookout for the tops of the tents, Hem," I said. "If we don't see any in a while, we'll turn back and go the old way around the front of the motel."

But what we saw wasn't tents at all.

Chapter Eighteen

THEY WERE DEFINITELY old houses I could see peeking through the trees up ahead. But not good ones. They weren't just the used kind of old. They were the broken-up, forgotten kind of old. The kind that smelled like a closet in the basement.

The road we were on split off to the left and deadended with a sign: *Knotty Pine Luxury Cabins. Dorothy and Crawford Pine, proprietors.* That sign was painted like new, but everything around it seemed at least forty or fifty years old. All six of the cabins looked like the special eggs I'd tried to make for Hem last Easter. The ones where you get all the yolk out and the only thing left is some broken-up shell to paint. The luxury had leaked right out of the Knotty Pine cabins. All except for one of them.

The brown paint on it looked pretty new, like it

might have been done recently. The front porch was a lot like our old yard when we'd had the inside of our house dumped onto the grass. Only the porch had more order to it. The stacks of books and clothing and gadgets were neat and lined up perfectly with the sides of the porch. About a dozen tiny plastic sunflower windmills were poked into the dirt in front of the first step in a perfectly spaced line.

A wheelchair was parked up against the side of the house, and the ground was so uneven that the wheelchair was resting on only one of the big back wheels and the two tiny foot pedal wheels in front. Although it wasn't piled as high as usual with all her bits and pieces of stuff, I knew it was Dorothy's. Even before I saw Lorraine push open the screen door and come out on the porch.

She was sipping at something in a mug, and from the way she was slurping at it real quick like and licking the middle of her lips, I knew it had to be hot chocolate.

She raised her mug to me and sat down in a faded red kitchen chair. She nudged a bundled stack of magazines out of the way with her foot.

Then out came Randall, with Dorothy right behind him. Dorothy noticed the stack of magazines right away, and fixed them back the way they had been.

Randall's hot chocolate must not have been so hot, because he wore most of it on his chin, with a long trail of it running down the front of his shirt and onto his name tag.

"Hemingway!" Randall acted as if he hadn't seen us in months.

And Hemingway was plenty glad to see him. Especially since Randall was heading over to a nice big dirt pile at the side of the house. Complete with trucks and plywood ramps.

Dorothy scooted another chair over next to the screen door, and Lorraine motioned for me to sit down. She raised one eyebrow at me and nodded toward the hot chocolate.

I looked at Dorothy and knew that Mama would have an out-and-out fit if I took anything to eat or drink from someone we didn't really know.

Like before, Dorothy's eyes were going straight through into my thoughts, and she nodded like she knew. "It's instant." She jerked her thumb toward the box on the kitchen counter. "In individual packets."

She had a way of saying it that made me relax, and she didn't make me embarrassed to say no.

The screen door was closed, but the door into the cabin was wide open, and I could see the stove where she had cooked up that hot chocolate. It was shiny white with a silver chrome canopy that made a nice roof hanging over the top.

Dorothy followed my eyes to the refrigerator next to it, and she smiled. "Nineteen-thirty-four GE Monitor Top refrigerating machine." She propped the screen door open with a kitchen chair and walked over in front of the refrigerator. "Foot pedal here opens it."

It had four legs that looked like small horse's hooves at the bottom. She stepped on a tiny foot pedal attached to one of the front hooves, and the door popped open. She patted the round white barrel on the top. "This motor has only had to be repaired once. About forty years ago. Been running ever since." She pressed the door shut. "Sort of like me. I just keep on going."

There was something about her that made a person feel right when they were around her. Lorraine felt it, too. I could tell by the way her shoulders relaxed and her mouth went into a half-smile.

Mama always says there's no call for rudeness, so I peeked just my head in the door to take a look at that sparkling white kitchen. It looked like one that Mr. Atticus Finch from *To Kill a Mockingbird* might have had in his house. That housekeeper of his, Calpurnia, was like a family member, and I think she and Dorothy polished their kitchens in the same way. With love and hard work.

Only I wasn't so sure Calpurnia had all those boxes of cake mixes and cans of corn. They were in perfect stacks and rows under the kitchen window and beneath the table.

Dorothy followed my eyes with hers. "My Craw can't go without his creamed corn at dinner. And not a week goes by that Karen Lynn doesn't get a taste for one of my yellow cakes with white frosting."

I wasn't sure who she was talking about, but I'd have to ask later. The living room off to the left had really caught my eye. The walls were all shelves. Shelves stacked with books.

My breath caught up in the back part of my throat, and I wished Mama was with me right then. I wanted her eyes to be taking in all that I was seeing. She knew what it felt like to have all those words sitting out in front of you. Just waiting for you to go get them.

Dorothy pointed her chin toward me. "You're

someone who weaves a good story, all right," she said. "I knew it even before Randall and Lorraine told me about your poems."

Lorraine nodded.

"I saw you sitting at the table over to the motel." Dorothy held up her fingers like she was writing. "I could tell by the way you were looking down at your paper, there were words flowing out of you." Her own sentences hung in the air in front of her while she looked straight through into my head again. "You have a way," she said. "You have a way of making the right words tack on to that paper."

She made me feel like Mrs. Rodriguez did. Like they could erase Daddy's words out of my brain and make me write new ones.

Dorothy came back out to the porch and sat down in one of the kitchen chairs. She followed my eyes from her crowded porch to her cabin sign and back again.

She smiled. "You thought I lived outside, in my wheelchair, didn't you?"

I felt my face get hot, and I knew it was bright red. She'd taken my thoughts right out of my brain.

She shook her head. "It's all right. That's what most of them think." She waved her hand back over her shoulder. "Most of those people around and about the motel think I'm just a crazy old woman. They think I don't hear them talking about me, but I hear what they're saying." She laughed, but it was a sad laugh. "If folks don't like the way you look, they almost never take the time to find anything out about you. They just make up their own stories."

I thought about that wall of books and I knew I wanted to know her. I wanted to know what she carried around in her wheelchair and inside her head. I was thinking she might be the kind of person that could help me figure out some things. Like how to get myself back to school.

I looked at her real hard in the black parts of her eyes, and I knew I wanted her to know me, too. Before I even took the time to think, I saw my hands pulling my notebook out of my backpack and holding it out to her.

She took it without looking at me and opened it up to the first page. Her eyes moved back and forth across the paper, and sometimes they stopped and went back a ways to start over. Lorraine read over her shoulder, and every once in a while she'd point out a line to Dorothy. Neither one of them paid me any mind, but they'd look at each other and nod or raise an eyebrow or two.

Finally, Dorothy leaned back in her chair and closed her eyes. When she opened them again, she looked me dead in the middle of my face. "You have some God-given talent, that's what you got. I happen to know that Ms. Harper Lee would appreciate someone like you having her name."

I knew my poems were good, but I wasn't used to other people saying so. Usually when someone at school said something about them, I'd feel kind of happy and embarrassed at the same time. But with Dorothy and Lorraine, it was different. My mind started racing around, trying to write itself out another poem to give them. I wanted to put that look on their faces again. I wanted them to feel like I did when Mama read me Ms. Harper Lee's words for the first time. My body had been relaxed, but my mind had been wide awake, waiting to hear what came next.

"Mama says the storytelling seeped through into my bones, before I was even born." I looked over at Lorraine, and she put the palm of her hand on the cover of my notebook, as if it was glass.

"I'm pretty sure I got it directly from Mama. She read me the stories her mama read her. When she tells those stories to me, her words move in all around me. She used to write down some ideas of her own, too." I looked at Dorothy out of the corner of my eye, and I could tell she wanted me to keep talking.

I had told Hem I wasn't going to talk about Daddy for the rest of the day, but I couldn't help it. Bits and pieces about him started slowly trickling out.

"Daddy made fun of her so much, she stopped writing her stories down for a while," I said. "He laughed about how she spelled, and he loved to point out her mistakes."

They both looked at me, but no one said a word. Lorraine's eyes looked as if she automatically understood about Daddy. No one had ever mentioned her daddy. Maybe he was like mine. Gone. Saving up his poisonous words for anyone that would accidentally listen.

At first it felt as if I was telling someone else's story. Someone I didn't really know that well. There was something about the way they were listening, all quiet and thoughtful, that made me keep going.

"Daddy couldn't tell a story like Mama." I thought back to him sitting at the head of the kitchen table, laughing at Mama with her notebook and pieces of paper.

Dorothy looked at me so hard, I couldn't move if I'd wanted to. "Harper Lee, don't you ever let anyone tell you to stop moving that pen. Writing's like breathing for you."

I knew her to be right, but when I thought about Mama, I knew sometimes things got themselves in the way of breathing.

Chapter Nineteen

I STEPPED AROUND to the side of the cabin to see what Hem and Randall were up to.

"He sure knows his way around a dirt pile." Dorothy picked up a yellow bulldozer at the edge of the dirt. She turned it over in the air in front of her and stared into the middle of the sky as if she had changed channels and wasn't quite with us anymore.

Lorraine made her way to the other side of the dirt pile and sat down on the rickety steps of one of the worn-out cabins next door. It looked like when I'd seen a building demolished. Daddy had taken Hem and me to see it. He'd made Mama stay home and rest, because Flannery was getting ready to arrive.

We can't get too close. Daddy had held one arm around each of us. *They're going to use explosives and implode the building. It's going to fall in on itself from the inside out. Kind of like a flimsy old card house.* I remembered how I'd felt standing there with him— scared, but safe at the same time.

We'd stood up on a hill across from the building and we'd watched the whole thing from beginning to end. And he'd let Hem ask as many questions as he'd wanted. I can still feel his hand on my shoulder as we watched the building fold in on itself.

But that was a different Daddy then. Before the whiskey got in and made angry puddles in his brain. Before he stopped looking for construction jobs and left all the work for Mama to do.

Dorothy seemed to follow my eyes along the wobbly lines of the caved-in roofs. She pointed at them with the little yellow bulldozer. "County comes along every so often to make sure no one's trying to live there. They didn't care much about what was back here until I sold the property from the side road there up to the main road.

"My husband, Craw, kept things in perfect working order." She shook her head. "They say my property's an eyesore." She sucked in her bottom lip. "They can come up here and spout off at the mouth all they want, but this here's still my property. They can put up whatever they like on that pittance of land I sold 'em." She pointed off toward the motel. "Who wants that tiny bit of land next to the highway, anyway?" She put her hands up by her ears. "It's nowhere for people to sleep with all that noise going by at all hours."

I ran my eyes over her freshly painted cabin. "You keep that fixed up yourself?"

She shook her head. "I have someone that comes in once a month and looks things over. Same person for the last thirty-five years." She narrowed her eyes. "I don't much like people poking around my personal belongings."

I got a sick feeling when she said that. It made me think of all the things we'd left behind that got contaminated with that filthy Early stink.

But she sure did have a lot of stuff.

And again, just like she could get right into my head, she swept her hand back and forth in the air in front of her. "A place for everything, and everything in its place. There's a good use for everything."

Dorothy sure did like rows. Skinny green poles that I'd seen in some people's gardens were pushed into the dirt at one end of the dirt pile. They were in three perfectly spaced rows of five. But they didn't have the beginnings of a plant or vines of any sort attached to them. They all held stacks of things that Mama and Hem and me usually throw in the garbage bin.

One of the poles held plastic rings from soda cans. And one of them held milk jugs, the pole threading through the opening in the handle. Another had margarine containers, stacked up like little pillbox hats, a hole poked in the dead center of each one.

Dorothy flipped the front shovel of the bulldozer up and down. "My Karen Lynn used to love to play with this thing. She'd dig holes up to your elbow, and the vacation people were always complaining about her rooting up the flowers in front of the cabins."

Lorraine hugged her knees like she was used to hearing about Karen Lynn. She was a good listener, and she rocked forward on her toes to let Dorothy know she should go on.

Randall stepped out of the dirt pile, and Dorothy handed him the bulldozer. "They don't make them like these anymore. You can't buy these at the store."

He knelt and took up a big scoop of dirt at the edge of the pile.

Dorothy shook her head. "Can't wear that thing out." She bent down and helped Randall push a pile of moist dirt in Lorraine's direction. "My Karen Lynn didn't get much of a chance to wear anything out." She bowed her head and made a sign of the cross on herself like I'd seen Mama do sometimes. *Head, heart, shoulder, shoulder.*

"Why that car squeezed the breath out of Karen Lynn and Craw but still left air for me, I'll never know." Dorothy brushed off the palms of her hands on the front of her pants. "Took a good enough piece of my head, though."

She tipped her forehead down and parted the hair on the side of her head with her hands. A white scar had made a path where the hair had forgotten to grow back. "Took the stitches out myself." She straightened up and smoothed her hair back in place. "Took myself right out of that hospital, too." She shook her head. "Those doctors didn't know much forty years ago. Know even less now. *You got a pretty bad head injury, Mrs. Pine. You need to stay here in the hospital for a while.*"

She looked at me. "I had no business lolling about in that hospital. Who did they think was going to bury my husband and my daughter?"

I was pretty sure she didn't want me to answer, so I sat down next to Lorraine without saying anything.

Dorothy pointed over at the wheelchair. "Took that thing home with me, which turned out to be a good idea. Comes in handy when I have my dizzy spells."

She seemed to be coming up on one right then, because her knees were looking a bit wobbly.

I wondered what it would be like not to have even one ounce of family to catch you or to pick you back up again.

Randall came galloping out of the dirt pile as if she'd rung a bell for him and led her back to her own front porch. "Time to go," he said over his shoulder.

Lorraine got up and started heading past the cabins. I thought Hem would put up a fight about leaving the dirt pile, but he followed Lorraine.

I watched Dorothy as she sat up on the porch in one of her kitchen chairs. I wished she had Karen Lynn to check on her and to bring her some hot chocolate. Her eyes were closed, and her head rested softly against the screen part on the door. She looked like she was settled in and comfortable, so I put my backpack over my shoulder and followed everyone.

The right side of the split in the road continued around the other side of the cabins. The trees thickened up some, too, and every so often we had to walk around a bush that had forgotten there was a road there. Those sticker bushes pushed right up through the cracks in the old asphalt and trailed long prickly vines in patterns across the road.

"She talking about Karen Lynn?" Randall asked.

Lorraine nodded.

He shook his head. "I figured so. She always gets those wobbly knees when she starts talking about the car accident."

It wasn't that cold out, but I shivered. It was hard to think about Dorothy having her whole family gone like that. All at once. When Daddy left, we knew he could come back if he really wanted to. But Dorothy's family wasn't going to be climbing the steps to her porch ever again.

I looked at Lorraine. "All that shaking she does is probably from her heart beating so hard."

Lorraine squeezed her eyebrows together.

"Your heart has to work extra hard when it's beating for people that are gone." I thought again about Daddy and how his being gone was something entirely different.

Lorraine smiled part of a smile at me, and I could tell she knew about the different kinds of being gone.

Randall looked back toward the cabins. "She calls Lorraine Karen Lynn sometimes."

Lorraine nodded.

Randall took a deep breath. "Just when she gets real busy with things. She still makes dinner for her husband and Karen Lynn most every night."

Hemingway wrinkled his nose up. "Dead people can't eat."

"Usually me and Lorraine eat it," Randall said.

That made my heart hurt for Dorothy, and I felt kind of guilty about all that wishing I'd done. All that wishing that Daddy would never come back.

Hemingway kicked at a bundle of brown leaves left over from the fall. "This road lead back to the motel?"

Randall shook his head. "This road is from way before. Before there was any motel. It's from when it was just Dorothy's vacation cabins." He pointed up ahead. "The road stops pretty quick."

Hemingway looked where Randall was pointing and shaded his eyes. "We coming up on your tent house?"

"Almost. We have to walk a bit first." He grabbed Hem's wrist. "Come on. I'll show you."

Hemingway and Randall took off at a run,

weaving through the bushes and stickery vines. It was kind of nice to walk along in quiet, with Lorraine.

I felt as if there was more room in my brain since I'd been talking to Dorothy and Lorraine. My thoughts seemed more organized somehow. Like Dorothy's rows.

"You kind of look after Dorothy, don't you?" I shifted the strap of my backpack onto my other arm.

She nodded and slowed her feet down a little to wait for me.

"I look after Mama and Hem like that, too," I said.

She tilted her head to the side in a thinking way.

"I've always done it," I said. "Even before Daddy left. Daddy used to do it way back when, I suppose. But he got so he wasn't doing that good of a job at it. And Mama and Hem are the kind of people that need taking care of."

She bit her bottom lip and waited for me to go on.

"I think that fire of yours licked its flames every which way . . ." I paused in my words for a second and watched her face, hoping it was okay to mention it.

Her eyes stayed on me, so I kept going. "My

daddy used his whiskey that way. It tore into everything to the left and right of him. Me. Hem. Mama. The more he poured it, the more he wanted that whiskey. And the worse things got." I breathed out a ragged breath. "He's gone now, and most times, I'm plenty glad about it."

It felt strange to finally say it out loud, but it made my whole body relax.

She opened her mouth as if she was getting ready to say something, but then she closed it and got real sad about the eyes.

"Your daddy gone, too?" I almost didn't ask it, but I think she wanted me to.

She put two fingers up.

"Two years ago?" I asked. Randall was right. She didn't have to speak her words out loud once you got to know her awhile.

She pressed her lips together.

"Before the fire." I started to ask it as a question, but I knew it to be true when she lowered her eyes.

"Mama knows I'm good at taking care of things," I said. "But I think she forgets I can't be doing it all the time."

The corner of my notebook was poking its way

through my bag and into my side. "I know you and Randall are on a long school vacation right now."

She nodded and didn't seem to be upset by it.

"But the thing is," I said, "I'm not." I ran my hand along the strap of my backpack. "I think Mama's been forgetting that, and I think it's time she starts remembering."

Lorraine raised one eyebrow like she might not have been expecting me to talk about Mama like that.

"I'm not sure how I'm going to do it yet, but I'm going to get myself back to school." I patted my notebook through my backpack. "Tomorrow, if not sooner."

Chapter Twenty

Words are just one way
To get people to listen to you.
I can listen to Flannery
Without any words at all.
Her softness pops into my brain
At the best times.
It moves around inside my head
To cover up the sharp parts of Daddy
Like a fluffy peach-colored blanket.

LORRAINE READ the last line over my shoulder as I
wrote it in my notebook. I hoped the peach part
wouldn't make her upset, since it was the color of the
outside edges of a fire.

But she smiled a little and raised an eyebrow, like

she had when she'd read my poems on Dorothy's porch.

I put my pen down on a chunk of asphalt beside me. "Hem waits for Daddy every night."

Her eyes didn't have one bit of surprise in them.

"He doesn't understand why Daddy left, but Mama and me do." I twirled the pen in my fingers.

The tears came from way back inside my head, as if they'd been pooling up there for a good long time.

Lorraine tilted her head to the side, which I knew her to do when she was listening carefully. She handed me a skinny roll of toilet paper from her pocket, and she waited patiently.

My tears came in heavy bursts, shaking my whole body. Finally, they lost steam and left me with quick, gulping breaths.

I tore a few squares from the end and wiped at my face. "I saw the mean part of Daddy, but Hem didn't." I thought back to Daddy yelling at me from my doorway and flicking my light switch. "Daddy never got Hem up in the middle of the night with his carrying on. Just Mama and me." I shook my head. "Hem always pretended not to hear him."

I remembered going into Hem's room to make sure he was okay. He'd always be making like he was sleeping, with his eyes squeezed tight and his hands gripping the top edge of his blanket as if he was slipping off a cliff.

I put my hand up to my ear, surprised for a moment that I could still hear Daddy's voice ringing in my head.

Lorraine leaned forward and raised her eyebrows.

"Then Daddy got deeper and deeper into his angry until one day he wasn't Daddy anymore. His eye color even changed up. His eyes used to be green, like Hem's and mine. It was all that whiskey that turned them gray. Dark gray, like old concrete."

Lorraine nodded, because she was someone who understood about color.

I closed my eyes. "There was plenty of yelling going on that last day." I remembered how the wall had formed a perfect circle. A perfectly round hole where Daddy had punched his balled-up fist. "There was so much hollering going on that in the end I wasn't really sure if he went because Mama told him to go or if he just up and went on his own."

But Mama's voice had sounded different that day. It had been low and careful, like she was stepping around pieces of broken glass. *You take yourself out of here, Wayne.* She'd had one hand on the telephone and one hand on the silverware drawer. *I won't have you and your nasty drinking infecting my children anymore.*

Hem's face was clear in my mind as Daddy hurried toward his pickup, and it made my tears start up again. I wiped at my nose with the back of my wrist. "The thing is, Lorraine . . ."

She leaned in closer.

"I wanted him to leave," I said. "But what I really wanted was for him to say good-bye to me. It didn't even have to be words. Just a wave."

Daddy had locked eyes with Hem for half a second. But just with Hem. And Hemingway had stood at the top of the porch steps, his whole face looking scared and sad at the same time.

Daddy had pulled out of the driveway without looking both ways. "He was afraid the angry part of him would get too big, so he had to get away," I said.

Lorraine pressed her lips together and nodded.

"I don't really want him to come back." I couldn't believe I'd actually said the words out loud again. "'Cause he makes me get a big streak of angry inside of me, and I don't like feeling that way about anyone."

I thought for a minute maybe I'd said too much.

But she didn't look to be leaving. She smiled a slow smile. The kind that makes a person feel better about things. The kind I think Flannery might have ended up having.

"That was the first time Hem waited." I let out a long breath of air.

Lorraine just sat, her body still and quiet. She didn't push a person.

"Hem wouldn't come in off that porch. No one could make him. It was way after dark that night when Mama finally scooped him up and took him inside to his bed." I shook my head. "That boy was dead asleep right on that top step."

Clang!

Lorraine stood up real quick like and pointed in the direction of the metal ringing sound. The direction that Hemingway and Randall had gone.

"It sounds like they're throwing rocks at a stop sign." I grabbed my backpack and took off running down the broken-up road. All I needed was to have to explain to Mama a gash on the side of Hem's head.

As we hurried down the old road, the trees and sticker bushes around us were getting thinner. The road took a quick turn to the right and widened into what looked to be an old parking lot.

Hem was perched on top of a shopping cart, turned over on its side. From the looks of all the rust and the two missing wheels, I could tell it had been a while since that cart had held any groceries. He reached down and dropped a rock onto the top of a round pile beside him.

Randall was a pretty good shot, I had to admit. He hurled a rock at a low pole with a metal box on top. *Clang!*

Hem put two fists in the air above his head. "Three in a row! Go to the next ones." He pointed to a long row of metal poles in front of Randall.

Randall looked to be getting ready to hurl another one when Lorraine marched up to him and wrenched the rock right out of his hand. She grabbed it so hard it knocked him off-balance and into a tall cluster of weeds.

I could tell Randall knew better than to complain. Lorraine stood over him in that cluster of weeds and her eyes narrowed and darkened, as if she might be thinking about planting the rock right between his eyes.

"I'm *sorry*!" He stood up and brushed the dirt from the backside of his jeans. "I won't bother your precious theater anymore."

She kicked at a rock on the ground.

"I *said* I won't bother it again!" He walked back to the shopping cart, as if Hemingway could defend anyone against anything.

I finally figured out what I'd seen from the pool. The white flags blowing in the wind were actually the bits and pieces left over from the old movie screen.

"This here's a drive-in, Harper Lee!" Hem pointed up ahead.

The frame was all there, and I tried to imagine how it had once been, with a movie playing across the wide white screen.

Lorraine tried to right a speaker box on top of the pole next to her.

"Lorraine's going to fix it back the way it was." Randall was trying to talk nice to get back on her good side, but I could tell she wasn't having any of it. She wouldn't even point her face in his direction. She was going from pole to pole, trying to straighten the speaker boxes.

Hem pointed at the one next to his shopping cart. "Cars used to pull right up here and put the speaker in their window!" He acted like Randall had thought of it all himself.

I ran my eyes over the broken-up metal boxes with the frayed scraps of wire trailing out of them, and I wondered how Lorraine was going to go about fixing them.

Lorraine came back toward me and motioned for me to follow her.

Off to the left was a low stone building with a flat roof.

Randall and Hem ran ahead of us. "It's the projector house." Randall patted a ragged piece of plywood that had been nailed to the front.

It was a good thing neither one of them could read much, because there were some words painted on the side of those dirty white cinder blocks. The kind Mrs. Early and her sister liked to use.

Lorraine led me to a side door and looked to be getting ready to go on in when the door swung open with a hollow bang.

Chapter Twenty-one

I REMEMBERED THAT tangled black hair from somewhere. And when I saw the spear teeth, I remembered straightaway where I'd seen her. It was the girl
from the motel. The one with the pointy elbows
and the nasty Winnie Rae Early voice. She plowed
out of the projector house, elbows out, just like she
had barreled ahead of me into the end unit of the
motel.

"Get off my property." Her voice pointed at each
one of us, but she didn't look at any of us. "And don't
even *think* about going in my house when I'm gone."

Lorraine rolled her eyes at her.

"Who you talking to, Alma?" The tall, skinny
woman came out of the door behind Spear Teeth,
with a baby on her hip like at the motel.

Spear Teeth poked her nose up at the sky, which

made her teeth jut out even more. She grunted and went around the other side of the building.

"Alma's had a rough day." The woman had far too kind a voice to be Spear Teeth's mother, but she had the same long coal-black hair. "She had to get up early to pack."

She reached around to pick up the corner of an old baby car seat and dragged it along behind her.

"I'll get it." I picked up the seat, since she was carrying the baby and all, but I didn't want to have to talk to Alma again. The last thing I needed in my life was another Winnie Rae Early.

I looked down, hoping to avoid eye contact, and followed Spear Teeth's mom around the side of the building.

But Alma didn't even try to talk to me. She sat in the back seat of a tan station wagon. It was piled high with bags and boxes, with only a small space left open next to her for the baby's car seat.

"Wish us luck," Spear Teeth's mother said to the air above my head. She had those same worry lines like Mama had between her eyes, so I knew she was going to need every bit of luck she could muster.

"Where you going?" I knew it was just plain nosy, but I had to ask it.

"We're going to Massachusetts." She smiled back at Spear Teeth. "To my sister's house."

"She doesn't really want us to come!" Spear Teeth shouted from the back seat.

"Oh, it'll be fine." She was smiling with her mouth, but not with the rest of her face.

Alma gave the seat in front of her such a hard kick, I could see it jump forward. "Uncle Lloyd says he don't have room for any freeloaders!"

I wasn't for exact sure what "freeloader" meant, but I was pretty sure it meant they couldn't pay their rent. Like us.

"Thanks for helping, honey." Spear Teeth's mother gave me a little wave and set to work buckling the baby into her beat-up car seat.

I looked back at Spear Teeth. Real quick like. And I saw it in her eyes. Without really knowing me, she knew about me and about what had been traveling through my head lately.

I didn't want to end up nasty and angry at everyone like Alma. Like Daddy.

I needed to get back to school to show Mrs. Rodriguez my poems. It seemed so simple. I'd never put one thought into getting myself to school before. I hadn't had to figure out one thing about it. I just got up and went. How did it ever get so mixed up?

Alma's station wagon moved off across the weeds of the drive-in theater parking lot, and I headed back around the corner of the projection room.

Lorraine was trying to prop a torn-off piece of cardboard in front of one of the swears painted toward the bottom of the building. She held it in place with rocks and stood back to study it.

Randall tried to pull the piece of cardboard away, but his hand snapped right back when Lorraine gave him her glare. It was a lot like my Mrs. Rodriguez look that I gave Hem. It was plenty hard to do, because you had to squint your eyes up and make one eyebrow tilt up at the same time. The first time I saw Mrs. Rodriguez do it, I knew I had to practice it. You couldn't use it very often or it wouldn't have as much bang. It always made Hem freeze in his sneakers and pay attention, and I could see it worked on Randall, too.

Hemingway was tugging at the ragged piece of plywood nailed to the side of the building.

"Get away from there," I said. "I don't have time to be digging splinters out of your hands."

"This here's the snack bar." He pointed at the

172

plywood. "Me and Randall are going to see if there are any leftover hot dogs."

It made me sick to think about how old those hot dogs would be if there were any still back there.

He looked to be reaching back for the plywood until Lorraine gave him one of her hard glares. As soon as she stepped into his line of sight, he dropped his hands down to his sides and took two galloping side steps away from the building.

When I saw those eyes of hers, I knew I had the answer to my problem. It had been staring me in the face so hard, it was a wonder I hadn't thought of it straight off. Lorraine could watch Hem for me!

My stomach and head were fizzing like I'd had two or three cans of soda. By tomorrow morning, Mrs. Rodriguez could have my poems in her hands. I could almost feel my desk under my elbows and the dusty, slick linoleum under my feet.

I'd have to start out plenty early, since they weren't about to let me on the school bus without the papers from Mama. But I could walk it. If I didn't have Hem with me, I knew I could. If I started getting Hem ready after Mama left, I could have him dropped off with Lorraine and get myself to school with time to spare.

Before I even went over to ask her, I knew she'd say yes. Bits and pieces of her reminded me of Mama. Lorraine was the sort of person you could count on. The sort of person that would stick around and take another job when the rent money ran out.

She smiled at me when I asked her, in a serious way, as if she knew right off how important it was to me.

"I could try to come back home at lunch." I turned and searched out Hemingway, off by the projection house. "He can be a handful sometimes, but he'll do what you tell him."

She shook her head when I said the lunch part, and waved the air in front of her like it was no big deal.

It felt as if my poems were burning a hole right through my backpack, they were so aching to get read.

"I really need to be getting Hem back to the motel." I pointed across the parking lot. "I'm thinking we need to head that way?"

Lorraine looked at Randall, and he nodded. "You can follow us to the tents, then you'll know the rest of the way back, right?"

I grabbed her hand. "Thank you so much, Lorraine. I don't know what I'd do without you."

She patted my backpack and led the way between the rows of speakers.

The only thing I was worried about was the path past the pool. Especially if Hem had it in his mind to do some begging. I had to get back and get my poems ready for Mrs. Rodriguez. I wouldn't have time for him to stop off and take a dip in the swimming pool.

But it turned out I had nothing to worry about. As soon as we left Randall and Lorraine off at their tent, Hem picked up the pace. It was time to do his waiting, and he was looking anxious. I didn't tell him he was staying with Lorraine and Randall in the morning. He'd be all excited, and he might let it slip to Mama. She didn't know them like I did, and I was thinking she'd never be letting me drop Hemingway off with people she hadn't spent time with.

"Hurry up!" Hem had picked his legs up to a good trot, and it was getting hard to keep up with him. He didn't even stop and try to take a swing on the old swing set in back of the motel.

As we went around to the front, I could see Mama's car in front of our motel room. I should have been excited to see her, but the feeling I got was one I'd been having a lot lately. The feeling that something wasn't quite right.

Chapter Twenty-two

OUR CAR LOOKED like Spear Teeth Alma's, what with all of the boxes piled on the seats.

Hem didn't even bother going inside the motel room, he was so anxious to get started with his waiting. His shoulders didn't relax until he was settled in solid on the chunk of concrete holding up the light pole at the edge of the parking lot.

When I opened the door, Mama was on the floor, putting together a U-Haul box.

"Mama?" I sat beside her, but she wouldn't look at me dead-on.

She tipped her forehead down and shook her head from side to side. The tops of her cheeks were wet. "I lost my job today, Harper."

The entire top half of my body felt like it was too big for me. Too heavy to hold up. I put my arm through hers like she did sometimes with me. "Oh, Mama. You'll get yourself another one. You always do."

I wanted her to agree with me, but the way her face was pointing to the floor told me different.

She shook her head slowly and finally looked up at me. "My three-day-a-week job went to live with her sister. It was where I made most of my money." She pushed the box to the side. "Not even a day's notice."

Mama finally looked me dead-on in the centers of my eyes. "We can't stay here."

My backpack felt like it had chunks of concrete in it. The poetry contest was in two days. Mrs. Rodriguez would never see my poems. I liked to picture myself reading my poems or one of my short stories up on the stage at the microphone. But right then I was having a hard time even remembering Mrs. Rodriguez's face or what the classroom looked like from my desk.

I had tried my very best to keep it away, but it was as if Daddy's poison had snuck itself on in anyway. And I felt like I was Lorraine. Like someone had gone and snatched away my words.

She bit her lip and started loading another box. "We need to get packed up so we can get out of here."

"We getting a house?" I knew it was crazy, but I

needed to stop her words from coming. Somehow, I thought if I could stop her words I could stop what was going to happen next. So I kept going without taking a breath. "Apartments can be real nice. I don't mind if it's small. We could even live on the top floor. 'Cause I don't mind stairs. Neither does Hem. That would give him a good place to do his waiting."

None of what I was saying made sense even to me, but I was afraid to stop talking. Afraid to leave Mama room to speak.

She stared out the window. "The night's not so cold now. It's warm enough for the car. And it won't go on forever."

I tried to imagine how it would feel sleeping on the seat of our car. I'd be sniffing in the old lady smell of Daddy's mama all night long. I was liable to start smelling like that.

I'd seen someone doing that before. Sleeping in their car. A whole family of red-haired kids. They had been parked in the side lot at the gas station. I'd tried not to look at them straight-on, because I'd been embarrassed to see them like that. Especially the one that had looked exactly like the girl that used to sit at the cafeteria table next to mine at school.

Mama spoke slowly, as if she was choosing each

word, one at a time. "Houses and apartments cost money. You need first and last months' rent and a damage deposit, right up front." She counted each thing off on her fingers. "And you need deposits for the electric company and the phone company."

"But you got some money saved up, right?" My voice was getting louder, but I couldn't help it. "And you've got those half-off coupons from Mrs. Early." I closed my eyes and tried to push away the picture that was nudging itself into my mind. Hem curled up in the corner of the back seat, looking grubby and uncombed like the red-haired kids.

Mama took a deep breath and let it out in quick, jagged bursts of air. "Mrs. Early is charging me half off the motel room here." She pressed her lips together hard. "But she's having me pay her the difference and then some."

"What?" That didn't make sense. There was too much to wrap my mind around. I needed her to stop talking. Everything was moving too fast.

She picked up her little figuring notepad and flipped through the pages. "I get half off the room, but I have to pay her a certain amount each week to go toward the rent we owe her from the house."

A sharp, hot kind of mean filled me. I was angry at

a whole bunch of people at once. Daddy, Mrs. Early—even Winnie Rae. But then it trickled out through my shoulders, where my backpack was, and made me feel like I did when I was back at the hospital, wishing for Flannery to open her eyes. Like maybe if I closed my own eyes and didn't think about it so hard, the bad things would change directions and go away.

I looked out the window and I could see Hem's rounded shoulders from the back. I knew he was feeling the same sort of thing.

Mama tried to smile at me, and she slowly rocked herself onto the balls of her feet and stood up. "I'm going to wash my face. Some nice cool water always helps to clear my head."

She shut the bathroom door behind her, and I scooted back against the bed, trying to clear my own head.

Mama's figuring notepad lay on the floor beside me. I knew she wouldn't take well to me flipping through her money lists and figures, but I couldn't help myself. I had always been good at math. Maybe if I looked through it a bit I could offer up some ideas.

When I flipped open the cover, my fingers felt rubbery, as if they couldn't quite get ahold of the pages. I didn't see numbers. I saw words. Mama's old writing. The writing she was too tired to do anymore. My face felt hot, but not the angry kind. It was the embarrassed kind.

I was ashamed at how I'd been feeling about Mama. All I'd been thinking about was the poetry contest, and here Mama wasn't even able to write down a single word. I might not be able to stand up at that microphone, but I could still pick up a pen whenever I wanted. I could write down a poem whenever it traveled through my head, but Mama didn't have the time or the energy even to put down a part of a sentence.

I flipped through the notebook until I found the numbers. When Mama picked up a pen these days, all she had the time for was trying to make the numbers add up right. I thought about how she used to look, perched up on a cushion, with her notebook resting on the arm of the couch. I hadn't seen that quiet, thinking look on her face in months.

I wanted to see Mama's face the way it used to be. The way her eyebrows squished together when she was searching for the right word to put down. And how her eyes got shiny and wide when she read Hem and me a good sentence or two. Those words of hers made me feel warm and comfortable.

Mama came out of the bathroom. Her face was clear, but her eyes were red and droopy. She gave me the kind of hug where you don't let go for a while. I breathed in her Mama smell. It was like clean cotton towels, fresh out of the dryer.

I hugged her back and I didn't let go for a while. So she'd know I wasn't going to give her a hard time anymore.

"I'll be right back." I ran out the door and over to Hem's light pole.

He looked up. "I heard a few trucks go by," he said. "But none of them slowed down to turn in." He pushed at a rock with his toe.

My heart went down to my feet, but I made myself start talking. "You know, Hem." I hated to say it, but I had to. Somebody had to. "He might not be ready to come back here. Not for a long while."

I wished so bad I could go and change Daddy for him.

He looked at me, kind of sad like, but he didn't seem to be getting ready to cry. "I know."

I was sad enough for both of us, but I was proud of him, too. He seemed a lot older than six right then.

"And it's Mama who needs our help right now, right?"

He nodded.

I held my hand out to him. "So come on. We got some boxes to pack up."

I made Hem practice his face before we went back in. Mama didn't need any more sad or angry in front of her.

He hung back against the light pole.

I put my hand out toward him. "Come on, Hem. Mama needs us."

He squeezed his eyebrows together. "You still mad about the rocks?"

The rocks at the drive-in seemed like hours ago. "No," I said. "It's fine."

He pushed off the light pole and started to follow me. "I wished there was at least some old candy left," he said.

I stopped and stared at him, because I realized he was talking about the projection house. The empty projection house.

I ran ahead into the motel room and picked up an empty box. "Listen, Mama," I said. "You might already have a few ideas in your head for us, but I want you to see something. Let's finish getting these boxes packed up, because I think you might like it."

Chapter Twenty-three

I WAS GLAD Lorraine had put the cardboard over the swears, because I didn't want that to be the first thing Mama saw when we drove up.

"What you got up your sleeve there, Harper Lee? This doesn't even seem like a proper road." She steered the sedan slowly over the cracks in the pavement. The road got so narrow in places that the sticker bushes were brushing against my side of the car.

"It's a real road, Mama, I promise. It's just old."

She looked to be getting ready to stop, but I knew she must've been thinking there was nowhere to turn the car around, so she kept driving.

We came up to the fork in the road for Dorothy's house, and I pointed the other way. "To the right, Mama. We need to go down there a little ways."

Finally, we got to the old parking lot. "See there? That little house? Just pull right up to the front."

Mama steered the sedan around the rows of drive-in speakers and pulled up to the old projection house.

She turned off the engine and sat back in her seat.

"I know it doesn't look like much," I said, "but wait until you see the inside."

"It's a drive-in movie theater!" Hem said it like he'd thought of it himself.

We got out of the car, and I saw Mama take in a deep breath of air.

It smelled wonderful out here, I had to admit. Lots of fresh, unused air. The sun was low, and it made the ground look like it was streaked with gold where the grass was trying to come up through the cracked asphalt.

The door was still wide open, the way Alma's mom had left it. I could tell from the way Mama was hanging back that she wasn't expecting to go inside. That's when I started to get nervous. Here I was showing Mama our new home, and I hadn't even set one foot inside the door.

"The person that was living here just moved out." I hoped Alma's mom was a decent housekeeper. If there was one thing that would turn Mama right around and send her back out the door for good, it was dirt and grime.

"Don't go in there!" Hem grabbed my arm as I was making my way through the door.

I shook his hand off. "What's wrong?"

"That girl, Alma!" He made his top teeth stick out as far as he could. "She said to stay out of her house!"

I didn't bother reminding him that he and Randall had already been rooting around inside the snack bar. "It's not hers, Hem. And she's up and left, anyway." I wasn't sure exactly who the place did belong to, but I couldn't let myself think about that right then.

The inside was dim, and you had to wait for your eyes to adjust. But what I saw didn't look half bad. It wasn't as nice as the Knotty Pine Deluxe Motor Hotel, but Alma's family had definitely fixed it up.

"Look there, Mama." I pointed to the two big mattresses pushed up against the side wall. "It looks plenty comfortable for sleeping."

I saw her eyes move up and down and around the entire inside. And I could see a bit of a smile in one corner of her mouth when she looked at the concrete floor. It was swept clean.

But I still wasn't sure we'd be staying until I saw her carry in the three-legged stool that her daddy had built. She put that carefully beside one of the mattresses and laid out Flannery's peach sweater across the top of the stool.

I headed toward the doorway to pick up a load from the car before she could change her mind.

She stopped me on my way out and put her hands on my shoulders. "It's just for now, Harper Lee. We need a roof over our heads, and I need a safe place for you and Hem while I look for another job." She looked out the door at the car, and her voice got shaky. "I know you can't be staying in the car all day, taking care of Hem, while I go to my job at the Laundromat and go out to look for more work."

I made myself smile. "It'll be fine, Mama." I pointed inside. "And it sure does seem clean."

Mama squeezed my shoulders and went out to the car for some boxes.

We emptied the car out fast, and Mama made the mattresses up with our bedspreads from the old house, the white chenille ones that had belonged to her mama.

She had never let us eat in our beds before, but Mama made us thick peanut-butter sandwiches, and we all sat down smack-dab in the middle of one of the bedspreads to eat them.

I didn't know why, but that peanut butter tasted extra good right then. It tasted so good, I even ate Hem's crusts for him.

Hem must've felt like it was special, too, because he didn't crumb up the chenille bedspread at all.

Then, without any hint of a warning, a memory of the old Daddy popped up in the front of my mind, and that safe, happy feeling disappeared into the concrete beneath me.

Mama and Daddy and Hem and me had all gone to the state fair. Daddy'd let us use up the last of the money he'd brought, so we could ride the Scrambler two more times each. I could still feel how the front of my face tried to make its way over by my ear as the Scrambler whipped us around and around.

Hem was remembering, too, because he took a bite of his sandwich and started whipping his head around. "Remember when Daddy took us to the fair and we used up all our supper money on rides?" He rubbed his belly. "It was way past dinner, and I forgot I was hungry until I got off the ride."

Mama smiled. But her eyes looked as if she'd lost something important and she couldn't begin to think on where to look for it. "And your daddy pulled that big bag of peanuts out of nowhere. Heaven knows where he got them."

Hem chewed his sandwich slowly in a remembering way. "Those were some good peanuts."

Mama closed her eyes. "He was always saving the day back then." She shook her head. "You'd think all was lost, and he'd come through with something or another."

I tried to remember how I'd felt that day on the Scrambler, but it kept getting drowned out in a Kentucky-whiskey puddle.

Hem looked toward the door and nudged me with his elbow. "What if Alma comes back?" He licked a spot of peanut butter off the side of his wrist. "She looks like the kicking type."

I thought about her pointy elbows and looked around the room. Before we had brought in our stuff, it had been pretty near bare, except for the mattresses. No pillows or even a book or a box of crackers. "They're not coming back," I said. "When people pack up their car like that, it's for good. They're moving on." That was something I knew for sure.

Mama pointed toward the door. "From the looks of things outside, especially, whoever owned this place hasn't been around for five or ten years. Maybe longer."

I wondered if we could still show ourselves a movie here, if we wanted to. I thought about how exciting it would be to set up the movie and sit out front in lawn chairs. We could still see bits and pieces on the bigger parts of the shredded-up screen. And we'd be able to hear it if we sat ourselves next to one of Lorraine's speakers. We'd invite Lorraine and Randall and Dorothy. I was so enjoying myself, I wouldn't even have minded a couple of old hot dogs from the snack bar.

Mama brushed off her lap and walked across the room to the counter that used to be the snack bar. What looked like a tiny garage door was cut into the wall above the counter. She reached for a rusted-up handle and tried to push the door up. "If I can get a good hold of this, I could push it up a bit and get some more light in."

I looked back behind the mattresses. The only two windows in the place were small and up high. Even though they let some light in, they were too high to see out of.

Mama finally gave up on the snack-bar window and stepped back. She pointed above her head.

"There are tracks that probably need to be oiled. It's supposed to ride up and over my head when it's all the way open."

I pictured people lined up outside at the counter. Ordering big boxes of popcorn and those long ropes of licorice.

If Lorraine fixed this up to be a drive-in movie theater again, she'd have to put a new counter on the outside. The inside one was sturdy and whole, but there wasn't much left of the part that had stuck through to the outside. There were whole chunks torn off, and a couple of swears scrawled across what was left.

Mama ran her finger along the inside counter and smiled full-on, because her finger came up clean.

She went to our boxes along the back wall and started opening the tops until she found the right one. Then she brought out her favorite picture. It was my favorite, too. Daddy had taken it about two years ago, when I was in the third grade. Hem and I were on either side of Mama, and she was reading to us from her special book. She had the front cover open, which meant she was on page one. I had this real excited look around my eyebrows, because I knew what was coming up. I was excited about Ms. Harper Lee's words.

Mama wiped at the front of the picture with the bottom of her shirt and set it carefully on the counter. Right in the middle, where we could all see it from our mattresses.

I scooted backward on the chenille bedspread so my back was against the wall, and I took out my notebook. My pen was moving almost before I could get my paper ready.

Home is kind of funny.
You can walk in your house
When you've been gone awhile
And it doesn't seem like it's yours.
Your things don't feel right.
They don't feel like they belong to you
Until you've been settled back in for awhile.
But a new place can feel like yours right away.
You don't need any settling-in time
When you've got your mama and your brother
And your favorite book.

Chapter Twenty-four

I FELT MAMA kiss my cheek, but I kept my eyes closed tight. That way it was easier to pretend things were how I wanted them to be. The truth was, I wasn't even sure what that was anymore.

Mama rested her hand on the side of my face for a moment and pulled the bedspread up so I could feel the bumpy chenille brushing my chin. Her footsteps were soft across the concrete floor, and I listened to the door opening and closing with a dull thud behind her.

I tried to make myself go back to sleep, but my poems were edging themselves into my head. It was the last day of school before the poetry contest.

I sat up and scooted to the edge of my mattress. Everything in me still wanted to get back to my desk and Mrs. Rodriguez.

I couldn't wait out another day with Hem. Then I

caught sight of my backpack leaning up against the wall, and I realized something plain and clear. The only thing that had really changed since yesterday was where we were sleeping. Lorraine could still watch Hem, and I could still make it to my classroom.

I got dressed and took everything out of my backpack, repacking it carefully. I even put in an extra peanut-butter sandwich for energy. I'd have to leave real early, so I could go find Lorraine first.

But it turned out I didn't have to. Hem had barely changed out of his pajamas when Randall showed up at the door. It was kind of strange the way he found us right away, just like at the motel.

I looked behind him. "Where's Lorraine?" I was a little nervous about what she'd think when she saw us living here. It would be hard for her to be turning it back into a drive-in movie theater with our stuff all around.

Randall walked by me, as if he was used to going inside. "She's coming." He carried a plastic grocery bag to the middle of the concrete floor and set it down beside Hem.

"Connect Four!" Hemingway pulled it out of the beat-up grocery bag and right away started setting it up.

"You know how to play?" Randall looked suspicious. "I'd better tell you, 'cause your rules might not be the same as mine."

I watched him take some of the game pieces back out of where Hemingway had put them. Randall definitely seemed like the type that made up his own rules.

Hemingway looked over toward the boxes. "Which one has my Chutes and Ladders?"

"Don't you be touching those boxes till Mama gets back. She'll have a fit if you mess things up." I secretly hoped the Chutes and Ladders had been left in Winnie Rae's camper. That game could go on forever and ever.

"When's she coming back?" He spun around on his bottom on the concrete floor.

"Not for a while." I went to the door to look out for Lorraine. "When she finishes up at the Laundromat, she's going to go try to scare up some more housecleaning jobs."

Hem got up and handed me my backpack. "Give him my good ones. He said he'd help, and he'll know the best places to put them." He pointed at Randall.

I shook my head and unzipped my backpack. I had thought Hem and I had settled some things about Daddy back at the light pole. But by bedtime last night, it was as if Hemingway had gone and forgotten every word of that conversation. I took out the maps he had been working on. Maps for Daddy, to show him how to get to the drive-in from the Knotty Pine Deluxe Motor Hotel.

Randall studied the map. "I know exactly where to put these. But I might need a few extra, in case it rains or something."

Hemingway nodded. "You can help me make some more later."

I looked out the door again, and I could see Lorraine walking through the rows of speakers. It was taking her a while, because she stopped every so often to right a speaker that had fallen off its post.

When she got to the door, I saw she was carrying a purple canvas totebag. It was decorated all fancy and glittery with puffy fabric paint, and I could see her sketchpad sticking out of the top.

She held up her totebag in one hand and picked up my backpack in the other hand. She held them side by side and smiled.

"That'd be great." I led her over to one of the chenille bedspreads, and we scooted back so we were under the windows, where the light came in. The way I'd figured it, I had a good half hour before I needed to get started walking.

I settled in and had begun putting myself in the mind of a new poem when Lorraine reached for my notebook and handed me her sketchbook and a couple of thin markers.

I shook my head and laughed. "I'm not much for drawing."

"Can't even draw one of those stick people," Hem piped up from the floor.

But she smiled and pushed the pad at me anyway.

I put it in my lap and rolled one of the markers between my palms. "I can doodle. You know, nice borders and such."

She flipped through my notebook.

"The blank pages are all the way in the back." Normally I wouldn't have let a soul put a pen to the page in my notebook. But Lorraine was different somehow. I didn't know why, but her putting a few words down didn't bother me a bit.

"It's okay with your mama that you stay here for a while?" I looked at Hem.

She nodded, but her hands were fluttery, as if her mind was nervous.

Randall looked up from the game. "It's a good thing you moved way out here, because Mama said we shouldn't be spending too much time around the motel today. The man from the state was poking around there yesterday, and Mama will get in trouble like last time if he finds us."

"The man from the state?" I didn't like how that sounded.

"Mama says he's from Family Services," he said, "and she said you should probably watch out for him, too. Dorothy said she thought she saw him looking in your direction when he pulled into the parking lot yesterday."

Lorraine nodded, her eyes wide.

"If he finds out you don't live in a regular house, he'll think your mama's not taking care of her kids right and he'll make a whole lot of trouble for her." Randall said it like he knew. And when I saw Lorraine's nervous fingers, I was sure it was the kind of trouble Mama didn't need.

The picture of Mama reading her special book stared at me from the counter, and I knew I couldn't do that to her. I thought about what Winnie Rae had said about the school nurse calling our house, and I got that same queasy feeling in the pit of my stomach. Yesterday I had promised myself I'd make things easier on Mama. And here I was getting ready to go off and make things worse.

Yesterday I had practically been able to smell the metal on the microphone up on the stage. But just now I could see it had gone and rusted itself up. I was going to miss that poetry contest for the second year in a row, and my insides hurt all the way from the middle of my heart down to the bones of my writing hand.

But when Mama's face looked back at me from the picture, I knew what was more important. As much as it hurt not to be in that contest, it would hurt a million times worse for our family to go crumbling every which way.

I leaned in close to Lorraine and lowered my voice. "I don't need you to watch Hem anymore."

She didn't act one bit surprised by what I said. She just nodded in that thinking way she had.

The Whaley County Poetry Contest permission slip peeked out of my notebook like a waving flag. Just glancing at that light blue paper made last night's peanut butter lump up in my stomach. The kids at school were most likely waiting their turn in the school auditorium. They always made everyone get up and practice reading in front of people the day before.

I made myself look at the picture again, because I was supposed to be up at that microphone.

My poems tumbled around inside my head, like they were begging for me to say the words.

I tried real hard to erase the picture in my mind of Winnie Rae Early spouting off her half-thought-out nonsense words at the microphone. She always tried to make hers rhyme. Anyone who knows anything knows it doesn't have to rhyme to be a poem.

Lorraine followed my eyes and tucked the paper back in between the pages of my notebook.

"It's okay," I said. "Really." But I knew before my words were even out, they weren't convincing anybody. Especially not Lorraine.

She put one finger up, and a slow smile crept onto her face. She rooted around in her totebag and took her sketchbook back from me. Then she bent down over a blank page and didn't look up until she was all the way finished.

When she finally held it up for me to see, I knew she had her mama's art talent, same as I had Mama's talent for words.

The words and sentences in my head slowed down a little and let me take in a nice long breath of air.

Lorraine's lettering was better than Mrs. Rodriguez's, and the swirl-and-dot design she had thought up for the border made your eyes not want to ever look away. The purples and reds traveled across the page in bursts of color, like on the batik cloth in Lorraine's tent.

"It's perfect," I said.

I glanced back at the picture of Mama, and this time my heart let me look at it straight-on.

Lorraine and I both knew it wasn't the same as being up on that stage reading for the whole school, but my poems wouldn't be sitting by themselves in my backpack, either. People would be listening.

Knotty Pine Luxury Cabins
Poetry Reading
Saturday at 11:00 a.m.
Don't miss this one-day-only event!
*Seating is limited, so arrive early
and bring a chair if you have one.*

Chapter Twenty-five

I WAS GLAD Mama had thought to take the toilet paper from the roll at the Knotty Pine Deluxe Motor Hotel. Lorraine and I were so busy making posters, I didn't have time to be thinking about toilet tissue when I went out back by the trees.

Hem loved going to the bathroom outside. It was going to be hard to break him of that habit once we got an inside bathroom again.

I tried to hide the roll under my arm as I walked past Randall to go outside. But he zeroed in on it right away.

"Why don't you just use the bathroom in here?" He pointed to the door in the back corner.

I shook my head. "No water." He was one of those kids that asked a lot of questions. No wonder

Lorraine didn't talk. She'd probably used up all her words explaining things to him.

Hem had tried to use the inside bathroom last night, but Mama had put a stop to it straightaway. She said the plumbing probably hadn't been up and going in those pipes for years. Spear Teeth's mother had kept both toilet stalls and the sink squeaky clean, though, even though they weren't usable.

Lorraine was waiting at the door with her totebag when I got back. She took out a hand towel and a big plastic water bottle. It was the kind of bottle that you might attach to your bicycle. You could squirt water in your mouth without stopping to unscrew the top.

She put one hand out in front of her and flipped it palm-up to palm-down. Then she pointed at my hands and held the water bottle over them. She gave them a good squirt on both sides and handed me her hand towel.

"You're used to going in an outside bathroom, aren't you?" I dried my hands and gave her back the towel.

She smiled and reached for one of my hands. She brought my fingernails up in front of her face and shook her head.

"I know." I put my hand behind my back. "I never let them get that dirty."

Lorraine put one finger up and leaned her head in the door. She held her water bottle up and pretended to be writing on a piece of paper with the other hand.

"I just took a shower yesterday!" Randall came out with a handful of maps.

She pointed at me.

"Oh, okay." He poked his head in the door. "Hemingway! Get yourself a towel."

Lorraine tugged on his shirt.

Randall nodded. "And some fresh clothes!"

She looked at me and nodded toward the door.

"We can't go swimming now," I said. "We've still got to hang up the posters."

Randall pushed past me and took a drink from Lorraine's water bottle. "We're not going to the pool. Lorraine's signing you up for the shower."

I was thinking maybe their mother had rigged up some sort of bathtub in their tent, until we got back to the Knotty Pine Deluxe Motor Hotel and we were standing outside the door of Room 12. The end unit that I used to think was theirs.

Dorothy came across the parking lot, pushing her

wheelchair. She studied her clipboard for a minute and looked up at me. "You're in luck today, because I've had a 'no-show.'" She put down her clipboard and let it hang from the string at the back of her wheelchair. "The rules are, you can take no longer than eight minutes per person. There should be soap inside, but you have to bring your own shampoo."

I nodded.

"Best thing is to sign up for next time before you leave today," she said. "That way, I get you on the schedule." She handed me her clipboard and a pen.

I looked down at the blocks of times on the paper and put Mama's name in for tomorrow morning. "What if the room gets rented on the day that I'm signed up?"

"It won't." She jerked her thumb toward the door. "Lock's been broken for a good two years now."

She pointed at Lorraine and Randall. "You two stick close to me while you're waiting. I'm keeping my eyes peeled for that dark gray station wagon." She turned to Hem and me. "And you two had best be staying out of the way of that social worker, too. I could've sworn I saw him looking at you two from across the parking lot."

I swallowed hard.

The door to the end unit opened, and a man came out towel-drying his hair.

He nodded at both Dorothy and me, and she motioned for me to pass him the clipboard.

"Hi, Mr. Corey." Randall smiled at him.

"Tell your mother thank you for the cheese she left." He nodded at Randall and Lorraine and chose his next time on the clipboard. "It'll last me through into next week."

I knew I recognized him from somewhere, and then I remembered he was the man with the square red tent the next one over from Lorraine and Randall. He was the guy who sat in the brown plaid armchair under the tree and read his newspaper.

Lorraine pulled a poster out of her totebag and held it up for Dorothy and Mr. Corey.

Dorothy took it and tapped her finger on the front. "This is a fine idea. A little literature will do us well around here."

I reached for another poster and handed it to Mr. Corey. "Will you put this on your tree?"

He nodded. "No problem." He made a little bow to Hem and me and walked back the way we'd come.

Dorothy put the poster under her arm and took the clipboard back. "You'd better get a move on if you and your brother want to keep your spot." She looked at me and pointed at the door. "The hot-water heater runs out after a while, and I need to give it some time to heat up again."

"I'll get the water going for you." I handed Hem the shampoo. "I'll keep the door cracked, and you yell for me when you're done."

Randall held up some of Hemingway's maps. "Me and Lorraine will go hang these up while we're waiting." Each one was folded carefully in the middle, and they'd gotten me to write *Mr. Wayne Morgan* in big letters across the back of each one.

I laid Hem's towel next to the tub and held his arm while he climbed into the shower. "Don't you be moving around a lot in there. I don't need you to be slipping and getting yourself hurt."

Hem was in the habit of sitting down in a regular old bathtub. He wasn't used to a stand-up shower, so I kept the door to the outside wide open. I made him sing the whole time so I'd know he was okay.

He was singing the jingle from his favorite soap commercial at the top of his lungs when I saw her a couple of units down. She looked at me straight-on and stared for a good while, so there was no mistaking that she'd seen me.

I stepped back into the end unit and yelled for Hem. "Hold on in there! I'll be right back!" And I ran across the parking lot to warn Dorothy.

Chapter Twenty-six

"YOU'RE TALKING ABOUT Ione Early, aren't you?" Dorothy didn't look to be in any hurry to get out of sight. "She's the one that's never bothered to have the lock repaired. Never put the work order in. She looks the other way when folks go in to use the shower."

I snuck a quick peek at Mrs. Early out of the corner of my eye.

"Who do you think left this clipboard out to begin with?" Dorothy asked.

It was hard to imagine. It was hard to believe even a thread of kindness had found itself inside anything Early.

"Your turn, Harper Lee!" Hem stood at the door, still wrapped in his towel.

"You turn off the water all by yourself?" I pulled the door shut behind me to keep the cold air out.

But I could hear the water on full blast in the bathroom.

He smiled at me. "I left it on for you."

I smoothed my hand over his wet hair. "You make sure you listen closely for Randall and Dorothy. I want to get a good head start back to the drive-in if they catch sight of that gray station wagon."

It felt good to take a shower and put on clean clothes. I made sure to use the inside toilet before I left, too. Who knew how long it would be before I'd get to use one again.

Randall and Lorraine were waiting for us when we came out.

"Dorothy said we could practice on her porch!" Randall held up a sketchbook. It was like Lorraine's, except smaller and more beat-up. "Me and Hem are going to show around our drawings in between your poems, and we might read a couple pages from *We Ride and Play.*"

When we got to Dorothy's, everybody made themselves comfortable on the porch.

"Everyone's got to stand up to practice," I said. "You've got to pretend like it's the real thing." I tried not to think about the microphone on the stage in the auditorium. It was nice of Dorothy to let us use her porch and all, but my whole body ached for that school auditorium and to hear my poems sound out all the way to the back row. I had been waiting for that contest for so long, I could practically hear my voice echoing off the auditorium walls.

But the funny thing was, when I closed my eyes to go over my first poem, it was hard to imagine myself there at the school. And when I opened my eyes and looked around the porch at Hem and Lorraine and Randall, I knew this was where I was supposed to be.

"Y'all haven't started without me, have you?" Dorothy dragged over a kitchen chair and sat back against the screen door. "Which one are you going to start with?"

"I think I'm going to let the poem choose itself." I held up my notebook and let it fall open to a page. "It's more natural that way."

I looked over the page a moment, took a deep breath, and started to read.

Bad things never
Stay bad for long.
They can be taken
Right over by something good.
The thing is,
You've got to be watching out
For those good things.
They tend to sneak up on you
And they can pass you right on by
If you're not on the lookout for them.

I read until my voice was raspy. The more I read, and the more they all listened, the happier I felt. I'd never felt better about my poems in all my life. Somehow, up on that porch, I just knew. My words were fine, and there was nothing Daddy or even Winnie Rae Early could do to change that. I wondered if I would've felt that way somewhere else besides Dorothy's porch. Like the school auditorium.

When I saw Lorraine hugging herself and Dorothy closing her eyes with a quiet smile on her face, I knew my words had been waiting around for something more important than the school poetry contest. They had been waiting around for someone who would really care about them. Someone like Lorraine and Dorothy.

Dorothy stood up slowly. "I'm going to go make up some of my date bread for tomorrow. Everyone used to love my date bread."

Hem and I went back to the drive-in to wait for Mama. With all the good luck floating around today, she was bound to have found herself a big house-cleaning job. One that paid enough to let her have a day off once in a while.

Chapter Twenty-seven

THE BAD NEWS arrived right along with the good the next morning. Mama hadn't found herself another housecleaning job yet, but she wasn't leaving right away. She was going to take a couple of hours off from her looking to come listen to me read my poems on Dorothy's porch. She had gone over to the motel first thing. She said she wanted to take her shower and get herself all gussied up for the performance. I couldn't wait to see her face when I was reading my poems.

Hem and I were decorating the fold-up lawn chair for her to sit in. I wanted everything to be perfect for her.

"Mama will be the guest of honor." I pulled apart a big brown paper grocery bag and tore it into thin strips. "Here." I handed a couple of strips to Hem. "Color some designs on these. Some zigzags and some stars. We're going to wind these through the armrests and fancy up the lawn chair for Mama."

Hem rooted around in his shoebox and pulled out a pointy blue crayon. "I was saving this for something special." He touched the point with his finger and put it to the paper, drawing a careful zigzag.

"Listen," I said to Hem. "You and Randall need to remember to look at your audience when you read. Mrs. Rodriguez says you need to look up every few words to let your audience know you mean business."

He nodded.

"Otherwise, their attention tends to wander, and they might just wander themselves right out of the performance." I hoped no one would get up and leave while I was reading. I wasn't at all sure who was going to show up. We had put posters up everywhere.

My fingers felt shaky as I thought about flipping through my poetry notebook. I hadn't read in front of more than one or two people before, and those people were usually just Hem and Mama.

At least I knew that Mama would stick around until the end. And so would Hem and Lorraine and Randall. And Dorothy. I wanted Mama to get a look through Dorothy's screen door. I wanted her to see Dorothy's walls of books.

Hem bent low over a strip of grocery bag and moved his crayon in a careful swirl.

"Get a move on there." I took the strip from him and wound it around an armrest. "We need to get this over to Dorothy's so Mama can have herself a front-row seat."

I picked the chair up from behind. "We can't fold it together or we'll tear the decorations." I kicked a crayon out of the way and headed toward the door.

"Wait!" Hem ran back to his backpack and grabbed *We Ride and Play*. He had managed to memorize the entire first story. All six pages.

We took some time getting to Dorothy's. I wasn't taking any chances in ruining the chair. I wanted Mama to feel special sitting in that chair while she listened to Hem and me read.

We were just about there when I saw the red and blue lights.

"Police cars!" Hem got excited and went into a trot.

But it was the ambulance I was noticing. The back door was wide open, and the drivers were lifting in one of those skinny stretchers on wheels. I could see straightaway who they had strapped to the stretcher, and my breath caught in my throat. I'd have recognized that pink stocking cap anywhere.

I dropped the lawn chair and took off behind Hem.

Randall was crying and trying to climb into the ambulance in back of the stretcher.

"I'm sorry, son." The tallest ambulance guy put his arm out to stop Randall. "No kids allowed in the aid car."

Randall had Dorothy's suit jacket in his hand. The one that looked as if it had belonged to Dorothy's dead husband. "She needs it." His voice came out small and squeaky.

Seeing Randall like that made my eyes pool up as I scanned the area around the ambulance for Lorraine.

She finally came around to the back of the ambulance and took the jacket from Randall. She stood head to head with the other ambulance guy and pushed right past him, climbing up into the ambulance. She unfolded the suit jacket over Dorothy and smoothed it out carefully over her stomach. Then she put her face down next to Dorothy's so their cheeks were touching.

I rubbed at my eyes with the back of my hand and tried to swallow over the dry spot in the back of my throat.

Randall was a lot stronger than he looked. He pushed a shoulder into the other ambulance guy and almost got past him.

Lorraine looked back at me, her face all blotchy and her eyes wide. "Hold him. Grab his hand. Please?" Her voice was low and raspy, and I wasn't even sure it belonged to her at first.

I couldn't believe there were real words coming out of Lorraine's mouth. My brain was trying to match those raspy sounds to her. Whenever I had imagined her voice in my head, it had always seemed more like mine. But her eyes were definitely the same, and they were telling me to listen to what she was saying.

I grabbed hold of Randall's arm good and tight.

"Go on, now," I whispered to Hem. "Get yourself out of the way."

Lorraine squeezed Dorothy's hand. "Come on, Dorothy. Please!" Her voice was still scratchy, but it was louder this time, and it got my tears going full-force.

I caught a good look at Dorothy as the tall driver was closing the back door, and right then I knew why no one seemed to be in any hurry. As nice as Lorraine had smoothed out that suit jacket, Dorothy didn't need it.

In that quick second, my whole body got cold.

Dorothy was gone.

I gulped back some air and wished it was like on TV, where in the next moment I'd see her eyes flutter open.

But the peach part was gone from her cheeks, and her eyelids didn't move.

I pulled Hemingway and Randall up onto the porch and watched the ambulance pull away. It rolled slowly across the rocks beside the dirt pile, as if it was taking care not to jostle its insides.

I wanted to run after it and sit with Lorraine. I wanted to help her get out the right words for Dorothy.

But instead I pointed the boys toward the kitchen chairs on the porch and scooted Dorothy's chair between them. I sat myself down in that chair and leaned back against the screen, like Dorothy had done when she was listening to my poems. She had made her way into my poems, and I wasn't ready for her to leave.

I saw Randall's wide eyes, and a fresh batch of tears ran down my own face. Lorraine's voice came back to me, with its rough scratchiness. In all the times I'd tried to think of ways to help her find her words, this wasn't how I'd imagined they'd spill out.

Everything felt different up there on that porch. The last few minutes hadn't seemed real to me. And now it was as if everything had slowed down.

I wished I could back everything up to yesterday and make it all go in a different direction.

Randall's voice was shaky when he finally spoke, kind of like when Lorraine first found her words. "She was sitting underneath the tree when we got here." He pointed across the yard at a toppled-over lawn chair. "I thought she was taking a nap." He sniffed in hard and wiped at his nose with the back of his hand. "But Lorraine knew something was wrong." He stared at the air above my head, like he was remembering. "Lorraine said her face looked too quiet."

I remembered Dorothy's face under that pink stocking cap, and I knew there wasn't anything Randall or Lorraine could've done. My whole heart hurt for Lorraine and Randall. I didn't want them to have to feel that Flannery kind of sad.

Then Randall worked himself up to a full-fledged cry.

Hemingway scooted closer and patted him a couple of times on the back, but I could see he didn't quite know what to do.

Neither did I. I gave Randall a couple of pats myself, but then I decided to let him cry. Sometimes a person needs to let it out until they're bone dry. I watched his shoulders shaking and tried to make myself think back to Flannery. I tried to think of the right words.

Lorraine's totebag leaned up against the porch on the other side of the door. I reached inside for my poems and sat back to read the one that seemed most fitting. The one I was working on when I first saw Dorothy Pine outside the motel room. I cleared my throat and read loudly, so loudly as to make those words reach after Dorothy.

Also Known As Harper

by Harper Lee Morgan

I have been Harper Lee Morgan
Mostly all of my life.
The way I figure
That name has soaked itself into my bones.
Lately, though,
I've been figuring on something different.
Something without the Daddy part hooked on.
Being just plain Harper Lee
Might help my brother know
It's time to come in from that long wait on the porch.
Being just plain Harper Lee
Might help my mama know
It's not her fault Flannery never opened her eyes.
It'd be nice to start out fresh
Without the ragged part of me
Tagging along behind.

I hadn't been paying much attention to what was happening out front of the porch, until I heard the clapping. Mama stood to the side, the kindness in her eyes reaching out to me. That face of hers always made you feel better no matter what was happening inside yourself.

Seeing Mama in front of me like that softened up the sharp edges inside of me.

I flipped through my notebook to look for the perfect poem, just for Mama this time, but I couldn't seem to concentrate.

I could see something spinning off to the side of the porch. When I leaned out, I saw Dorothy's clipboard hanging by a string from a handle of her wheelchair.

I remembered how carefully she'd written my name so Hem and me could have a warm shower. The fresh running water had felt so good. Just thinking about that made my tears get going again, rolling down my cheeks like the shower water.

I looked at Mama. "I'll be right back."

Chapter Twenty-eight

THE PARKING LOT of the motel was empty, except for Mrs. Early's cart. It sat in front of our old motel room, folded sheets piled high on top, and all her cleaning bottles dangling from the side.

Dorothy's voice made its way into the front of my brain and reminded me of why I was there. *She's the one that's never bothered to have the lock repaired. She looks the other way when folks go in to use the shower. Who do you think left this clipboard out to begin with?*

I knew Dorothy wouldn't want all those people missing their warm water. I had to give the clipboard to Mrs. Early. She'd know what to do with it.

I hugged the clipboard to me and looked in the window of our old room. The woman straightening up the velvet horse painting reminded me straightaway of

Mrs. Early, without the extra-large part. When she turned more to the side, I saw she was Winnie Rae's aunt, mother of the truck stealer from our old dirt pile.

I moved quickly to the next window, hoping real hard she hadn't seen me. That's when I heard all the crying and carrying on. It sounded suspiciously like Winnie Rae Early, and it was coming from the direction of the end unit.

I was pretty good at sniffing out the Early stink, and wouldn't you know, there she was, blubbering away on the floor of the bathroom.

She had wedged herself down between the bathtub and the sink, and her crying was the kind where you forget to take a breath for a while.

I took a couple of steps in and stopped. "You hurt?" I wasn't used to this kind of Winnie Rae. A mean Early was so much easier to deal with than a crying one.

She seemed more like Hem's age, all hunched over like that. She wore pink patent-leather sandals with glittery jewels on the straps and her toes pointed in toward each other.

She looked up from behind her knees and took a big hiccupping gulp of air. I knew that not to be a hurt cry at all. It wasn't the kind you let out when you've taken a fall on the pavement. It was a sad kind.

It was the inside kind of hurt that doesn't plan on letting up for a good while.

"What happened?" I ducked down by the sink so I could understand her hiccupping words better.

"Birdie." That was the only clear word I could get out of her.

"Who in the world is Birdie?" I didn't know what was wrong with Winnie Rae, and I needed to find her mama and get back to wait for Lorraine.

I didn't have time for her blubbering. Why should I, when she hadn't even taken the time to explain to Mrs. Rodriguez where I was? I could still hear Winnie Rae's nastiness in my mind. *I told Mrs. Rodriguez you're not sick. You just don't live there no more.* She loved telling me how the teacher was skipping over my desk.

I picked myself up and started to head for the door. My feet wanted to take me right out of there, and just leave Winnie Rae sobbing her eyes out in the bathroom.

But that sad crying of hers was swirling around me, and I couldn't stand seeing her hunched over like a hurt animal in a corner. That kind of hurt had taken hold of me before, and I knew I had to try to help. Even if it was Winnie Rae Early I was helping. It was the gasping that got to me most, and without my thinking much more about it, my feet turned themselves around and took me back to her.

I put my hands on my hips. "You're going to have to tell me what's wrong, and you're going to have to tell me who Birdie is, Winnie Rae Early, or I'm turning around right now."

She looked up at me. "My mama's baby came today." The words were so quiet, it was hard to believe they were coming from Winnie Rae.

"Your mama's at the hospital?" I squatted down next to her.

She wiped at her nose with the back of her hand.

"It was too early." Her voice made my stomach feel hollow. It made me remember what my whole family tried not to think about.

"What?" I narrowed my eyes at her.

"She wasn't supposed to come yet." She looked down at her fancy pink sandals. "It wasn't time. She needed to wait for three more months."

Finally, I knew exactly what she was saying.

Birdie was her mama's baby, and she'd forgotten to open her eyes.

Like Flannery.

Somehow, I must've forgotten it was Winnie Rae, because, the next thing I knew, I had my arm around her.

"She didn't open her eyes?" That baby-wipe smell was coming back to me like I was in Mama's hospital room again.

Winnie Rae looked at me. "She opened them." She rubbed at a corner of her own eye. "They were gray. Birdie's eyes were gray."

I nodded. "Just like yours."

"Mama put a little pink hat on her." She held her hands up to show me how small it was. "It was the one that I bought. It had a tiny white bow in the front."

I thought about Flannery's peach sweater, and I knew Winnie Rae and her mama were never going to forget about that little hat with the tiny bow.

"Mama said Birdie didn't know how to breathe yet. Her lungs weren't all the way finished." She took in a long breath of air, as if she was trying to do Birdie's breathing for her.

I scooted closer, so our toes were almost touching. "Listen here, Winnie Rae. I know about babies who never quite are."

She looked me dead-on in the middles of my eyes.

"Because of Flannery." And before I knew what was happening, some of the Flannery sadness crept up into the corners of my eyes.

"A baby?" She looked at me real confused, and

that was a Winnie Rae I wasn't in the least bit used to. The one I knew always acted as if she knew it all.

It was hard to look at her when everything that was coming out of her eyes was running down her face and mixing up with the mess that was coming out of her nose.

"I guess I didn't know you that good back then." I reached over and pulled off a strip of toilet paper for her. "She never actually came home from the hospital with Mama."

Winnie Rae took a swipe at her face with the end of the toilet paper.

"She died." I don't think I'd ever said those words out loud, and it didn't even sound like my own voice when I was saying them.

I wiped at my eye with the back of my wrist. "What you're feeling like right now isn't going to go away for a while, that's for sure. So if you're wanting to talk some about Birdie . . ." I thought about Flannery's tiny fingernails, and my heart hurt in the deep-down corners. "If you're wanting to talk about Birdie, maybe we could do that once in a while."

She moved her head ever so slightly, but I was dead certain it was a nod.

I peeked my head out of the bathroom door, and I

could see the corner of the maid cart through the front window. "Your auntie's liable to come looking for you." I pulled at her arm. "And my mama and Lorraine and everybody are going to be wondering where I've gotten to."

The funny thing was, a poem was trying to write itself in my head right then. When a poem was trying to come out, there was never a whole lot I could do to stop it. The best thing to do was just write it down.

Words seem more important
When they come through a microphone.
It fancies them up somehow
As if they're not even
Yours anymore.
But I know what
Is really important
Is not where you're standing
When you say them.
It's the one special person
That's listening hard
To hear
What you have to say.

Chapter Twenty-nine

"I DON'T THINK the roots go much deeper than this."
I pulled at the little peach tree in my old front yard.

Lorraine took hold of the trunk beside me, and we
yanked it right out. "Dorothy loved fruit of any kind."

She glanced back over her shoulder for the mil-
lionth time.

"I'll tell you what, Lorraine," I said. "I don't
much care if any Earlys do happen by. I planted this
peach tree, and now it's going to be Dorothy's."

She set the tree in Dorothy's green wheelbarrow
and started to push it toward the road.

"Hold on there." I scooped the loose dirt back into
the hole and smoothed it out with the back of my
shovel. Then I took the forget-me-not seeds out of
my pocket and sprinkled them evenly over the patch
of dirt.

Lorraine looked at me and nodded, and we made our way back to Dorothy's.

Mama didn't say one word when we got back with that peach tree. And I was pretty sure I saw the corners of her mouth smiling. Hem and Randall already had the hole dug pretty deep over to the side of Dorothy's porch, and all we had to do was set the tree down in.

Mrs. Kelley, Randall and Lorraine's mama, stood next to Mama and smiled at the little tree. "You might just get some peaches from that tree next year." She sounded quite a bit like Lorraine, without the raspy voice. She sat on the bottom step of Dorothy's porch and smoothed her skirt over her legs. The skirt was blue and swirly, like the cloth that had covered my dresser in their tent.

Mama glanced back at Dorothy's house and smiled sadly at Mrs. Kelley. "I wish I'd had the time to get to know her."

Mrs. Kelley nodded. "She meant the world to us. Especially to Lorraine."

Lorraine looked over at Dorothy's wheelchair, parked in the corner of the porch. The string that used to hold the clipboard dangled from the handle and blew to the side in the breeze. She picked the clipboard up from the porch and held a pen out to me. "I know she'd like it if you and Hem took care of the sign-ups."

I took the pen and nodded. I could see Dorothy's face clear as day in my head, and those thinking lines she got about the eyes when she was concentrating on one of my poems. I was real happy to take care of something that was so important to her.

"She didn't like it when the schedule got messed up." Lorraine shook her head and smiled, as if she was remembering.

I clipped the pen to the paper on the clipboard and turned toward Dorothy's screen door. I half expected Dorothy herself to come walking out with her hot chocolate. I could see the tall piles of batik cloth, folded and stacked on her kitchen counter. It seemed strange to see Randall and Lorraine's tent taken apart and separated into individual pieces like that.

Mrs. Kelley patted Lorraine's hand. "She had no one after her husband and daughter died." She looked at Mama. "The lawyer said when she sold the property that the motel sits on that she never spent a dime of it, except what she absolutely needed to get by."

Hem tilted his nose up toward the sky. "She's got somebody else to take care of now."

I knew right away what Hem was talking about, because I'd been thinking the same thing. I just hoped she'd had enough time to get ready for a baby up there.

"What's Hem talking about?" Mama looked up in the sky, as if she was trying to see what he was seeing.

"He means Baby Early," I said.

Lorraine nodded. "Dorothy loved babies. She was always fawning all over the babies at the motel. She's definitely taking care of Birdie Early up there."

I scooted Dorothy's kitchen chair closer to Lorraine. "It was kind of hard to get used to the drive-in movie theater being Dorothy's. But you knew it all along, didn't you?"

Lorraine smiled a tiny smile, but her eyes got shiny.

Maybe that was why she'd wanted to fix it up so badly. She'd wanted to make things nice again. For Dorothy.

I knew Dorothy had needed Lorraine, just as much as Lorraine had needed her. And that's why Dorothy's lawyer said everything now belonged to the Kelleys—the house, the drive-in, even the swimming pool.

Dorothy had filled in all those wide spaces that were left when Lorraine lost her words.

Lorraine stood up and wandered over toward the dirt pile.

Mrs. Kelley took a deep breath. "We're going to take our time at the clinic up north. The doctors there know all about helping people like Lorraine who have been through terrible events. We'll be away for at least six months. Probably longer."

I finally had someone who was better than just a school friend, and here she was, up and leaving. Six months seemed so long. I had to keep reminding myself that it wasn't forever. She'd be coming back.

I looked at Mrs. Kelley. "They want to make sure she keeps her words?"

She nodded.

Mama ran her hand along the side of Dorothy's kitchen chair. "We'll take good care of the house for you. I promise. Your letting us stay here will help us get a leg up."

Mrs. Kelley smiled. "You're the ones doing us a favor, believe me. It'll be worth the peace of mind I'll get, knowing someone is taking care of things." She looked toward the screen door.

I thought about that foot pedal that opened the

refrigerator door, and how we would think about Dorothy and Lorraine every time we cooked up some hot chocolate on the old stove.

And just as if Mama was reading my mind, she took my hand and said, "Maybe we'll have a new refrigerator of our own by next year."

"How about an old one with a foot pedal?" I knew that sometimes old things could be a lot more interesting than new ones.

Mrs. Kelley fished her car keys out of her pocketbook and stood up. "We'd better get a move on before the afternoon traffic starts up." She waved at Randall. He was digging a long trench in the dirt pile with Hem. "Come on, now, and say your good-byes!"

Even though we were living in the house that was now theirs, I needed to know for sure that they'd be back.

It was as if Lorraine had listened in on my thoughts, because she stood very still and looked at me straight-on. "I'm going to be thinking about you every day," she said.

I smiled my best smile, the one that leaks over into my eyes. "Me, too."

She put her hand out like she was stopping traffic. "Wait here."

She ran into the house and came out with a purple batik cloth. She shook it out and put it around my shoulders. "It's the first one I ever made."

I reached down into my backpack and brought out a little notebook. It was like Lorraine's sketchbook, only smaller. And I'd decorated the front and back with blue forget-me-nots.

I handed it to her. "They're all in there. I copied them in my best handwriting."

"Your poems?" She hugged the book close, and then she hugged me.

I pulled the cloth snug around my shoulders and felt the purple soak into me. "You know," I said, "your words were inside of you the whole time. Nothing was lost."

She ran her fingers over the blue forget-me-nots and flipped the cover open to the first page. She took her time walking to the car, reading the whole way.

Randall leaned over the back seat and waved out the rear window of the car, and Hem waved until he couldn't possibly see the car anymore.

And then he went and all-out surprised me. He turned back toward the dirt pile and took up his shovel.

I didn't mean to say it out loud, but the words

came out before I could catch them. "Isn't it time to do your waiting?"

"Maybe tomorrow." He looked over his shoulder at me real quick like and went back to his digging.

I let out a long breath of relief. Knowing Hem, by tomorrow he could be right back to doing his waiting, but I sure was happy that he was learning to take a day off.

"Okay, then." I dragged one of Dorothy's kitchen chairs off the porch and set it up next to the bottom step. Then I arranged the purple batik cloth over the top of the chair. In case Hem changed his mind, he would have a comfortable place to do his waiting.

I watched Hem play with Karen Lynn's bulldozer and thought how Dorothy was back with her family. Somehow thinking about all those Pines being together again made me feel all calm and quiet inside.

I sat down in the chair I'd fixed for Hem and thought I might feel the beginnings of a poem coming on.

But then those first words were stifled with a hint of something Early over my left shoulder. And as usual, I guess I smelled her before I saw her out of the corner of my eye. Winnie Rae Early stood at the edge of the lawn and looked to be searching for something to say.

"That lady died, Harper Lee Morgan." She put her hand on her hip like she was delivering up some fresh news. "My mama said she dropped dead not far from where you're standing."

"That so?" I was inclined to use some of the words from the side of the projection house on Winnie Rae, but they stuck there on the way-back part of my tongue, not making their way outside of my mouth. I kept thinking about little Birdie Early, and I decided to let Winnie Rae run on at the mouth as much as she wanted for now.

"That ain't your property, Harper Lee Morgan, and you know it." She pointed her nasty old voice in Hem's direction. "He oughtn't be digging holes in someone else's dirt pile. I might be forced to call the authorities."

I kind of liked it when Winnie Rae had the wrong information. It got downright funny when she spouted off like she was the only one who knew what was going on.

She looked over my left shoulder, in the direction of the little peach tree, and her mouth dropped partway open, like she might be getting it ready to say something. But I set my eyes on her in a quiet way, and she closed it right back up again.

"Take your nasty self off this property, Winnie Rae Early, and don't you bother coming back." But I didn't say it like I meant it.

Winnie Rae made like she was going to move off, but she folded her legs under her and sat down in a corner of the yard. She took some decks of cards out of a shopping bag and started arranging them on the grass beside her. She didn't look to be going anywhere for a good long while. We had some things to talk about now, and I think we both knew it.

Mama came to the door and motioned for me to come in.

"I *might* be back." I ran up the steps and turned my head in Winnie Rae's direction. "So don't you go messing up the yard."

Mama stood in the living room, in front of one of Dorothy's walls of books, and she had a tall stack on the floor next to her.

She pulled another one down and opened the front cover to show me something. "She was a professor, Harper. A professor of literature at a university." She pointed down at the stack of books. "Her name's in all of these: *Dr. Dorothy Pine.*"

I tried to picture Dorothy in teacher clothes in front of a class, like Mrs. Rodriguez, but it was hard to imagine her without her wheelchair and clipboard, or without her dead husband's suit jacket. The part I could see in my mind was her face when she talked about books, and the way she looked when she read my poems. The part of her that loved words and stories had never gone out of her. That had hung right on and stayed when everything else had changed for her.

Mama stood in front of that wall of books with a look on her face that I hadn't seen in a good long while. The look she had was both calm and happy at the same time. I hadn't thought I'd ever see that Mama again.

She took down another book and held it close to her. The soft cover was practically worn off of it, it had been opened so many times.

It didn't take me long to figure out what book it was. Mama sat down on Dorothy's velvety brown couch and patted the cushion next to her.

"I've been a little out of sorts lately, haven't I?" She put her hand over the book on her lap. "I always get a little out of sorts when I haven't had a good solid dose of Maycomb County, Alabama."

She smiled at me, but her eyes had a touch of

sadness in the inside corners. "I feel as if I have been away on a long trip."

"You didn't go anywhere, Mama," I said. "Your mind was working on other things sometimes, but you were right here with us." I patted her arm and watched the worry lines on her forehead smooth themselves out.

I closed my eyes and thought about the thirty-six tally marks on the wall next to the refrigerator in our old house. I wondered if someone had painted over them.

Mama opened the front cover of *To Kill a Mockingbird* and traced Dorothy's name lightly with the tip of her pointer finger. Then she took in a deep breath and got ready to read.

"Hold on a minute, Mama." I picked up a pencil from the table. That little table was the perfect size for writing on. And it had two chairs, one for me and one for Mama.

I leaned in toward Mama and opened my special notebook to the inside front cover. "You want to make the tally mark?"

I wondered how many times we'd get through Ms. Harper Lee's book before Lorraine and Randall got back.

Mama shook her head and smiled. "You do it, Harper."

I heard the screen door slam, and Hem came in and settled himself on the couch next to Mama.

I made that first tally mark all careful and straight, and I went over it a couple of times, to make sure it was going to stay there.

Mama and Hem snuggled close on the couch, and I wished I had someone to take our picture. But then I knew I didn't really need one. Mama and Hem with that book would always be fresh and clear in my mind. The place might need to change once in a while, but the part that was the same was the three of us. Together.

"Okay, I'm ready." I settled in on the other side of Mama. Then I closed my eyes and waited for the words.

Acknowledgments

The birth of a book is no small endeavor, and so many people have contributed, both knowingly and unknowingly, from start to finish. My sincere gratitude goes to:

- Andy, for that espresso you bring me every morning, for picking up the slack, and for being your awesome, sarcastic self;
- Jessica and Holly, who never cease to thrill and amaze me and, best of all, make me laugh;
- my incredible agent, Dan Lazar at Writers House, for his sense of humor, insight, and wise advice;
- the wonderful staff at Henry Holt, especially my brilliant editor, Reka Simonsen, for her gentle encouragement and uncanny ability to coax out the right words;
- my indefatigable critique group, Margaret Welch, Pam Farley, and Mary Jo Scott;

- Trish Nellermoe Byers, my first pen pal;
- Eileen Edwards, for always saying the writing was good;
- Pat Giff, for her time, kindness, and wisdom;
- Mary Rinear, who first called me a writer;
- my brother Tim Haywood, for making our childhood an adventure;
- my older brother, Tom Haywood, for so graciously/unwittingly appearing in my first book;
- Leslie Olson, who was there for the first novel;
- Rose Kent, who taught me perseverance;
- Johnny Kelley, my East Coast father, for his constant encouragement;
- Lorinda Haywood, who has so graciously dispelled the theory of the evil stepmother;
- the Village people on up to Roseleah, for their untiring friendships;
- Monique Johnson, Chris Pennenga, and the NEMAA people, who helped build the confidence that every writer needs.